I0684516

"Star Flight"

Part Two Of The

Intervening Years

Of The

Ic'nichi - Human Chronicles

An Ic'nichi Young Adult demi-novel
translated into human language

by,

Robert A. Boyd

Copyright 2015 by The Written Wyrd
All Rights Reserved

ISBN: 978-0-9862680-8-3

English Trade Paperback Edition

Proceeds from the sale of this work go to support self-published and small press authorship. If you wish to aid this effort, please go to your local on-line accessible bookstore, or to the publisher's website —

The-Written-Wyrd.org

— to purchase additional copies for friends and your local library.

Thank you.

§

This is a work of fiction. Any resemblance between the characters portrayed and actual persons, living or dead, is purely coincidental.

*****

For:

Link

A Note From The Human Translator

As with all Ic'nichi works, this book has certain terms which simply do not translate into human languages due to their odd nature. As has become a tradition in these things, an Addendum has been added in back to provide possible—rough—meanings. We hope the reader will understand and bear with us on this.

*****

"Being Called To Account"

For all the tough-fem image R'nemReth tried to show the world, she was scared. She was often scared—on the street, in the Peace Warden lockups, and more recently in the Remand Forum where the case against her was built step by step.

It wasn't fair! she thought, bitterly, for the umpteenth time. The Universe knotted her tail since she was hatched, blocking any hope of a normal life, and now she faced the final indignity. It wasn't her fault she was a misfit. It wasn't her fault the others in the crèche treated her like a freak. The youth councilors hounded her about her grades and how she didn't fit in, as if it was *her* fault the other younglings turned on her, abused her, made her a pariah.

Life in the crèche was miserable as far back as she could remember. She never did have any friends and the local bullies made each day a test of endurance. The few times she fought back, however poorly, earned her some brutal beatings and stern lectures from the councilors about her 'attitude'. Never mind that she was the victim: she was *expected* to 'blend in', to 'earn their respect'— the respect of vicious *un'tdars!*—and above all to quit getting into fights. Even at her tender age, she could tell they were clueless *n'bna'nmn* who merely went through the motions.

She finally fled the crèche, to take up the hard life of the streets. She learned, fast, how to survive. And survive she did; one of the 'lost herd' of troubled younglings. She learned how to take what she needed by guile and deception; proved to be very adept at it. But not adept enough.

They caught her with the goods eventually. It wasn't the first time the Peace Wardens cornered her, although she usually got away with a short term in a juvenile 'Readjustment Circle', which was a torment it its own right, before being sent back to the crèche, and escaping again. She had a reputation on the street as an uncommonly talented swindler, and unbeknown to her, the Law was watching. She was clearly more than just another of the 'lost herd'. So they followed her trail patiently, building their case step by step, waiting for her to make a fatal mistake. And make it she did.

They went to trial, and she knew enough of *Laws And Customs* to know they had her this time. The depth of their case unnerved her. The evidence against her was solid, and her appointed Council was unable to shake the witnesses. She knew enough of *Laws And Customs* that the verdict was no surprise. She was looking at *life* in a penal nest. She knew it was a foregone conclusion before the Civil Council rested his case. She was going away to some *Ancestorless* hole for a long, long time.

No, it wasn't fair at all. She was just trying to survive in a hostile world. She used to have such *beautiful* dreams of adventure, travel, success. She used to while away the lonely days longing for something forever beyond the horizon. Those dreams sustained her over time as her bitter reality consumed her. And now that she was old enough to be convicted as an habitual felon, even her dreams were being taken from her. She silently cursed her ill-luck and wondering why she was ever hatched in the first place.

§

They adjourned for the day after the verdict was read, and she was herded back to her cell to await sentencing the next day. It left her emotionally defeated. It shouldn't matter, really. Going to a penal nest would be a breeze after life on the mean streets of Xi'vrre'nmmemns Great Nest. At least she would be fed regularly, which would be a novel experience, and would face less risk of physical assault. Still, the idea scared her. Her cell in the local lockup felt like a tomb, smothering her until she felt she would go *er'trxxda*. The plain steel bars and Depressing Institutional Pale Green cement walls pressed in on her like a physical force until she wanted to scream in terror.

She heard the door at the end of the hall open long before the block Warden appeared in front of her cell. "You have a visitor."

That was a surprise. The verdict was read and sentencing wasn't due until tomorrow. It was already late; visiting time was nearly over and the food cart would be around soon with late-meal. And there was no one she knew who would bother to visit her here in the lockup.

"Who is it?"

"Don't know. Someone to see you." the block Warden couldn't care less about her or her troubles. "You want to see her or not?"

Her? It wasn't her council, then, which made the mystery all the more curious. There was nothing else to do, and nothing ahead of her but another night staring at the walls and feeling lost. She could use the break. "Might as well," she said, sullenly.

§

The block Warden took her to one of the interview cells: a bare room split by an unbreakable glass divider, with a functional seat cushion on either side of the barrier. She settled on the seat cushion and stared at the door on the far side, wondering who wanted to see her and longing to go through that door to freedom; if she even knew what freedom was any more.

A moment later the far door opened and her visitor came in. The sight caught her by surprise; she didn't recognize her, but she was obviously not someone off the street. This stranger was a *r'fen'thi,* middle aged, a bit plump but still most attractive, dressed in stylish, inexpensive clothing. She stopped in front of the glass partition and studied her for a long moment, and her aura was distressed, saddened. That made the mystery of her visitor all the more opaque.

"Hello, R'nemReth," she said, softly.

Her finely tuned empathy, her one edge on the street, gave off conflicting signals. "So who are you?"

The visitor's ears reclined in dismay at her tone. "We've never met before." She definitely seemed troubled. "I've watched you from afar since you hatched. I stayed away because I didn't want to interfere in your life."

"Wonderful. That tells me nothing."

"My name is C'traBenla."

"So? What's your story? Are you some kind of hatchling psychologist or something?"

"No. Actually...I'm your mother."

"My...mother? What does that mean?" She couldn't figure this fem out, which worried her.

"The word is a human term. We don't have an equivalent in our language."

7

"What? A human word?" This really didn't add up, and this stranger's aura of love and despair was confusing. "You came in here to play some kind of *p'quas'tka* game with me?" she snapped. "Well I'm not interested. I got more important things to do!"

"You are my hatchling."

It didn't register at first, and R'nemReth blinked at her in confusion. "What? Your hatchling? What is this *ui'DmukNa*?" Her temper was starting to boil up, and she tamped it down forcefully. The block Wardens were more than capable of slapping her down if she got out of hand.

The visitor shook her head. "No, no game. I really am your mother, and you really are my hatchling."

This was unheard of. None of those *n'bna'nmn* in the crèche knew their...mother. The world simply didn't work that way. Her egg was surrendered to the crèche shortly after delivery, as was done since time immemorial, and she was hatched and raised there like everyone else. She couldn't *imagine* actually keeping an egg and trying to raise a hatchling on her own.

"You got to be joking," she said, uneasily.

The stranger's ears drooped in sorrow. "No. No joke. I couldn't let you go, even though I knew the crèche in the World Nest would give you a good upbringing. I managed to follow your progress over the years—never mind how—until you ran away." The stranger sighed. "I lost track of you for the longest time until your name started turning up in the Peace Warden reports."

That in itself was a disturbing reveal. Peace Warden reports weren't for just any casual reader. Her having access told R'nemReth this C'traBenla, her supposed...mother...must have connections.

"Alright, so you found me. What of it?"

"I'm so sorry, R'nemReth!" C'traBenla cried. "I knew you were a troubled hatchling, but until you ran away, I had no idea how bad it was!" She pulled herself together with an effort. "What went wrong?"

"What went wrong? The whole *p'quas'tka* world went wrong! They all knotted my tail every chance they could, and the *un'tdar* instructors didn't do *p'quas'tka* about it!"

8

"Surely it wasn't that bad...?"

"What do you know? You've never had herds of vicious *un'tdars* after you! You've never been afraid to leave the dormitory, never been afraid to go to the cafeteria, never been afraid to be out of sight from one of the instructors. You never had to watch your tail constantly. You want to know what went wrong? *Everything* went wrong, from the moment I was hatched!"

C'traBenla's aura sank into bleak despair. "I'm so sorry, R'nemReth! I know hatchlings can be vicious *riv'Agna* but I didn't realize it was so bad!" The mental aura said someone in the crèche system was in for a tail-knotting. "I'll do whatever I can to help you."

That offered a glimmer of hope. "Then you can get me out of here! Get the conviction reversed!"

C'traBenla gave her a troubled look. "I...can't do that."

"*p'quas'tka* you can't! You have connections, I know you do! You couldn't access my files otherwise!"

That made her visitor nervous for some reason. "I have some influence...enough to find out what became of you. But I don't have that sort of grunt."

As suddenly as hope came, it was cruelly ripped away again. "Then what good are you? I've been convicted as an habitual felon. They're going to send me to a penal nest for *life!* If you can't get me out of here, then what good are you?"

"I...don't know. We can file an appeal..."

...She was interrupted when a large figure suddenly appeared out of nowhere, taking up much of the small room. It was a human, tall, heavy-set, with a dark brown, almost black hide and dirty white fur. C'traBenla reacted like she'd been stung, rearing back in amazement. "J J?" she gasped.

"Hey there, Baby-Chile," the big human said. "It's been a long time."

C'traBenla got over her surprise, and broke out in a rush of pleasure. "J J! It's good to see you again!"

"Ah'm happy t' see you too."

R'nemReth was shaken by the sudden appearance, and stared in wide-eyed amazement at this unexpected visitor. She's seen humans at a distance once or twice, but never had the chance to get up close. And up close like this she could feel something—*strange* —something *unnatural* about this intruder; a '*power*' she couldn't comprehend. The sensation set her scales crawling.

"But...I thought you weren't going to contact us any more?" C'traBenla said to him.

The stranger mused over it. "Well, no, that ain't quite so. We had t' take back them empathic powers 'cause you folks couldn't handle 'em, and that makes it hard t' connect to you-all, but ah nevah said we wouldn't come callin' again."

"Well you're certainly welcome. So...what brings you here?"

"Actually, ah'm here t' see about her." The stranger nodded in R'nemReth's direction. "She might have the fixin's fo' somethin' important."

R'nemReth was worried, not the least because his attention came with a spooky aura which made her *r'vebbe.* The way he looked at her sent a chill through her, and her finely tuned empathy, which served her so well on the street, was warning her this stranger was not *at all* what he seemed to be.

C'traBenla blinked at him in confusion, then looked back and forth between him and R'nemReth. "What? What do you mean? What do you want with my daughter?"

"She was still in th' egg when yo had them powers, and they's a residue of 'em still in her. That means maybe she can do what needs doin'." The big stranger radiated a sense of sincerity and concern which spooked R'nemReth almost as much as his original appearance. "It's all fo' the best, Baby-Chile. D'you trust ol' J J fo' this?"

It took C'traBenla a moment to collect her wits. "Well...yes, I trust you J J. But I don't understand. She has psychic powers?"

"She sho' does. She got the empath; it's one of the most basic of all powers, an' she got it good. Ah saw it in her when you came heah t' visit jus' now."

"What? Are you still linked to me?"

J J Ballas smiled awkwardly, and R'nemReth felt a wave of warm, slightly embarrassed emotion flow through her like a strong breeze. "Well, t' tell the truth, when we took them powers back, ah left just a tiny bit in each of you; you might call it a seed. That was so it'd be easier fo us t' reach out t' you again if we needed. Ah look in on you from time t' time, just to keep in touch."

"Really?" C'traBenla seemed surprised, if anything could be surprising by then. "Well, I suppose it's a good thing you happened to 'look in' when you did."

J J smiled again. "Actually, them seeds ah mentioned are supposed t' let me know if yo' psychic residue acts up...just in case you needed help, ya know. Yo' seed triggered when you came in heah wit' her."

C'traBenla stared at him in disbelief for a long moment. "Honestly I don't understand you, J J," she said, softly. "Your powers can be frightening at times."

"Ah know, Baby-Chile." The big stranger emitted an aura of regret. "Yo' minds jus' ain't equipped t' grasp us. We don't mean no harm by it."

R'nemReth shared C'traBenla's uneasiness, and then some. She always had an uncommon ability to understand what others thought and felt. She used her talent to survive, hustling ignorant *t'pithm'igs* who figured her for an innocent score. She never *imagined* in her wildest dreams that her empathy was implanted into her by a bizarre alien. And now it seemed this alien was here to collect, and from what she'd seen of his powers, whatever he wanted couldn't be good.

C'traBenla pulled herself together with an effort. "I do trust you. It's just..." She shook all over in a nervous fit. "So why did you come here now? What do you want with my hatchling?"

The stranger mused over R'nemReth for a bit. "Ah ain't exactly sure if she got what we need. Ah got a tingle when you came in heah, an' ah can feel her power." He mused some more. "But ah can't rightly say if she's got what'll be needed, though."

"Needed? Needed for what? What can she do?"

"That depends on what she can handle." The stranger turned to R'nemReth, and walked *through* the glass partition like it wasn't even there. She backed into the corner, cowering in fear as he studied her solemnly. His gaze met hers, and she felt the *oddest* sensation, like he was looking right into her mind, moving about

11

inside her head, examining her psyche. Her head pounded, and she gasped for breath. It was a *creepy* sensation which left her shaken.

He nodded at last, as if he made up his mind about something important. "Yeah, she'll do." He turned away, lifting the bizarre sensation from her mind, and walked through the barrier again. "They's a task fo' her," he said to C'traBenla. "It's an urgent task. She perfect fo' it, an' from what ah see, she could use the chance. You need t' set things in motion fo' her."

"Task? What task?" C'traBenla seemed confused. "What are you talking about?"

J J smiled at her. "Well that-there is an *inverse* cognitive function, don'tja know? Gotta go, Baby-Chile, can't stay no longer." And with that, he vanished into thin air.

"J J..." C'traBenla sagged in dismay, seemingly stunned by this bizarre appearance. After a moment she shook off her distraction and pulled herself together. "*p'quas'tka*, J J," she muttered. "What did you mean by that?"

R'nemReth stared stupidly at the spot where the stranger vanished. Her head ached, her hearts raced, and she was trembling. She fought to get herself under control, not altogether successfully. "How...how did he do that?" she asked at last. "I didn't know humans could just disappear."

"Actually, he isn't a human." C'traBenla seemed as perplexed as she was. "He's a Dreamsinger."

"A...what? A Dreamsinger?" R'nemReth remembered hearing about them sometime back. "That was some *other* kind of *alien?*"

"Yes." C'traBenla was shaken and distracted. "We first made contact with them over twenty years ago, well before you were conceived."

It was beginning to dawn on R'nemReth that the Peace Wardens should have stormed the room by now. She glanced at the security camera: didn't they notice a hulking black human appearing out of thin air in the middle of their secure complex?

"These Dreamsingers must be some strange *riv'Agna*."

C'traBenla offered a bemused ear twitch. "You have no idea."

Her headache was reaching horrific proportions. "Ancestors," she gasped. "I feel terrible."

"That's J J." Through her pain R'nemReth could tell C'traBenla was suffering too. "We can't handle psychic contact with them for more than moments."

"I...think I'm going to be sick..." And she was, although thankfully her stomach was empty. She was racked by dry heaves for some time, her head pounding in agony, before the spasms passed. "Ancestors..." she gasped. "You have...some *p'quas'tka* strange friends."

"Are you alright?"

She gave C'traBenla as much of a venomous glare as she could manage. "No, I'm not alright. I'll never be alright again." She struggled to her feet and flopped on the seat cushion. "What is it with you anyway? You come in here with some wild story about me being your hatchling, and you drag *him* along for the ride."

"I really am your mother, R'nemReth. I came here to see what I can do to help, which I guess isn't much. As for J J, that wasn't my idea. They tend to turn up at the oddest times, and they've always been a riddle."

The whole scene left R'nemReth shaken. "What did he mean about me having a task? What does he want with me?"

C'traBenla gave her a troubled look. "I honestly don't know. The Dreamsingers aren't very adept at explaining things to us non-empaths."

"Well I don't see any reason to perform any task for them! Not with *this* headache. He's got a real high-tailed attitude coming in here and...and...prying like he did."

"R'nemReth, J J Ballas and the Dreamsingers are strange beings. It's hard to relate to them, they're so different from us, but they aren't evil. We've dealt with them before, and they mean well, even if they have a hard time understanding us."

"And you *trust* him? H-he can walk through walls! He...he was inside my head...how do they do that?"

"Psychic powers. They depend on psi like we do speech, using our hands, just about everything we do physically. Trust me: what you saw was only a hint of what they're capable of."

"That's...really scary. Why does he look like a human, anyway?"

13

"They borrowed the image from the memories of a human. They use it to communicate with us. They come from a gas giant world, and they don't look anything like humans, or us."

"I don't want to know what they look like. I don't want anything to do with them."

"R'nemReth, he said you could use your empathy to do something important. This could be the answer you need to avoid going to a penal nest."

"Oh? How?" Not that R'nemReth cared just then, as miserable as she felt.

"I don't know. Maybe they'll reveal that later. The important thing is you may have a way out of this mess."

That gave her a faint sense of hope, the first she'd felt in a long time...but the price...what this J J Ballas wanted in return was not comforting to think about. "I wish I knew what this 'way out' will cost."

"No idea. The Dreamsingers can be a puzzle at times." C'traBenla shook her head, and her ears twitched her dismay. "*l'cc'vn,*" she muttered. "I wish they'd simply tell us what they wanted rather than playing these guessing-games."

Just as suddenly as he vanished, J J Ballas was back. "All yo need t' do, Baby-Chile, is ask the right person." He gave her a knowing blink of one eye. "You'll know who." Then he vanished again.

*****

"Setting A New Course"

Morning came as all her mornings came: bleak, cheerless, promising nothing but despair. She moved through her morning routine like a robot, resigned to the inevitable, trying not to think about what lay ahead...or the disturbing events of yesterday. The stray memory sent a chill through her. Did that actually happen? She never met an alien before, certainly not so up close and personal. She never *imagined* such powers could exist, or that they could alter her life so devastatingly.   It all seemed like a nightmare...maybe it was. It had to be. The only other explanation was she was going *er'trxxda*, or it really happened. She couldn't afford to believe either of those alternatives.

C'traBenla arrived at the lockup bright and early, turning up just before R'nemReth was about to be taken before the Justice, which shattered her fragile trust in the power of nightmares. The mal with her was bulky, muscular, middle-aged, with a hard expression. The look went with the 'Dark Grays' uniform he wore, which convinced the Wardens to give them a moment to visit even with the Forum already in session.

"R'nemReth..."   C'traBenla seemed nervous and unsure of herself for some reason.   "This is Ki-Elder I'eiBida, my bond-mate...and your father."

"My what?" She got a bad aura off this newcomer, which put her on her guard.

"It's another human term. He sired you. You're his hatchling too."

"So this is her?" the stranger grumbled.   "I don't see what all the fuss is about."

"I swear to you, I'ei, J J Ballas appeared to me, right here in this cell. She saw him too. He said she has an important task to perform."

The Ki-Elder shot a hard look at R'nemReth. "Is this true?"

"Uh...yes. There was this big human, all black-like...he popped in and popped out again just like magic."

That set his ears back, and she caught an aura of amazement from him. "What did you feel when you looked at him?"

"Um...there was...I don't know. He had this *aura*...really strange...like there was some sort of *energy* oozing out of him. And I could feel his moods, what his emotions were." She shuddered at the memory of the meeting. So it actually happened; she tasted rising fear. "And he...*looked* at me. It felt like...like he was looking right inside me. I felt him in my mind."

The Ki-Elder's ears reclined in dismay. "It *was* him." He turned to C'traBenla. "But why contact you now? No one's heard from them for sixteen years."

"He said R'nemReth has an important task to perform. He said she has a residue of the psychic powers they saddled us with while I was carrying her."

He pondered that, with a speculative look at R'nemReth. "So what does this have to do with anything?"

"I dug into her trial records." I'eiBida gave her a sharp look as she dug several pages out of her pouch. "She's a con-artist, really outstanding at it. Her psyche evaluation noted she has unusually high marks for empathy and manipulation. That must be what J J was talking about."

I'eiBida snatched the papers from her and pored over them. "So? From these accounts she's a complete misfit, a sociopath. Her record doesn't inspire confidence in her worth to society. I don't see what J J expects of her."

"I'ei, this is your *hatchling!* She was struggling to survive on the *streets!* Is it any wonder she did what she had to? The least you can do is offer her your support!"

R'nemReth could tell he was getting annoyed. "C'tra, she's a common criminal! I know it hurts, and I'm sorry you have to go through this, but you should never have kept track of her in the first place. She's been convicted on multiple counts of fraud and theft. She's destined for a penal nest, and there's nothing you can do to change it."

R'nemReth noticed he said 'you' rather than 'we', which said she couldn't count on him, not that C'traBenla didn't try. "She's a victim of circumstance! Can she help it if she's young and immature? J J can give her a way out of this mess, and it's up to us to figure out how."

I'eiBida sighed, and his ears reclined in dismay. "Not again," he muttered. "Wasn't one bad enough?"

C'traBenla was becoming frantic. "There's still a chance! If we can figure out what J J meant, it could give her a way to earn redemption!"

"There's nothing she can contribute!"

"There must be *something!* Otherwise J J wouldn't take an interest in her."

I'eiBida was going through the papers again. "In any event, she's to be sent to a penal nest. She isn't free to roam the streets regardless of reasons."

"Something off-world, then! There must be *some* urgent mission her psychic powers can be useful for."

The Ki-Elder faltered, then turned pale. "The Flyers?" he whispered. His aura changed abruptly from skepticism to confusion.

"That must be it," C'traBenla insisted. "It's off-world, and everything they tried thus far has failed."

Confusion changed back to skepticism. "Maybe so, but it's not like they *have* to succeed. We can simply quarantine the planet."

"That would be admitting defeat, I'ei, and you *hate* to admit defeat. She's a long shot, true, but maybe she can untie this cosmic tail-knot."

He mused over it, and skepticism faded to indecision again. "Maybe. But I don't understand what he's up to."

"This was J J's idea. With the Dreamsingers involved, who can say for sure about anything?"

His indecision was tinged with sudden fear, which made R'nemReth wonder why he was so worried. "There is that," he said. "But I still don't see what J J expects from her."

"How many times have you told me to leave things to the specialists?" she said, severely. "Trust J J to know what he's doing. They are the experts, after all."

He emitted a loud sigh, and his ears reclined in resignation. "My Ancestors must be having a grand laugh at me."

"No doubt. But remember you are *her* Ancestor, and if you are worthy of *them*, she should be worthy of *your* help."

He gave her a bleak look, and his aura became muddied. "I never could resist you, Ancestors help me," he mumbled. He brooded for a bit, then turned to R'nemReth. "You have a choice. If you are willing, I can get your sentence transferred off-world. It may give you a chance to redeem yourself."

"Off-world? Isn't a penal nest bad enough?"

"It won't be easy, or pleasant, but you might be able to do something essential. If you can, it could go a long way to giving you a new start."

"Why should I trust you?"

"Because I have more important things to do than play with you!" he snapped. "I don't have all day, so what'll it be?"

"You want me to go out into space, to some other world?" She was stunned by this unexpected turn of events. "That sounds dangerous. So what do I get in return?"

He bit back on his temper, and eyed her severely. "It is *conceivable* that if you achieve what we hope, a Writ of Forbearance could be arranged," he growled.

A Writ of Forbearance? That was her only hope of ever being free again, and from the look of him, he had the grunt to arrange it. She felt a surge of uncertain hope rising in her.

"Well..."

"Yes or no!" She was shaken by his stern, commanding tone.

"...yes..."

§

The block Warden came to take her before the Forum a bit later, and the two of them were already taking seats in the gallery when she arrived. Her Council met her there, and his aura was one of resignation. He eyed the two of them, making special note of I'eiBida's uniform. "What's with them?" he asked, quietly.

R'nemReth threw them a quick glance. "I'm their hatchling."

Her Council's aura lit up in confusion. "You're related to the Fleet First?"

"It seems." That was a bit of a surprise. She hadn't realized he was a minor legend: part of the original herd which opened the first embassy on earth, now field commander of the fleet in the event of war. Even she knew of his exploits.

He shook his head in amazement. "It takes all kinds." The Forum was getting under way, so he let it drop. R'nemReth took her place at the end of the line with her Council at her side. "I filed a petition for clemency in view of your age," he mumbled to her. "But I don't think it will do much good." As if to emphasize the point, the small Judgement Bell on the Justice's desk tolled out four times: another sentence passed. The line crept forward another space.

"What...if you file a petition saying I'm *er'trxxda?*" Her Council looked askance at her. "I just learned something," she added. "It may be grounds for dismissal."

Her Council sighed. "I'm afraid dismissal is out of the question. Petition *er'trxxda* has to be filed with the original challenge. In any event, being *er'trxxda* doesn't buy you anything. You'd only be sentenced to a psyche institution rather than a regular penal nest."

The Forum was soon busy, with various defendants and their Councils waiting their turn for sentencing. A few onlookers sat in the hard seat cushions behind the railing, with the Forum's Wardens spaced around the room ready to deal with any outbreak. The one thing missing was the four member Judgment Panel: this day was reserved for passing sentences for the convictions from the last several days; they were off prepping for other cases.

The bell rang four more times. The line crept forward another space. R'nemReth lapsed into silence, staring at the floor in front of her, lost in despair. Her life as she knew it was coming to an end. It wasn't much of a life, but at least she used to be free. Going to a penal nest would be better than the only life she had ever known, but the thought still made her miserable.

The bell tolled four times. The line moved forward.

She thought fleetingly about the unlikely offer from her two visitors...they were still squatting in the gallery. She hardly cared that she was the hatchling of a planetary hero; she felt nothing toward either of them anyway. But their offer...a chance to earn a Writ of Forbearance...but the price...

The bell tolled four times, sending a shiver through her. The line moved forward.

She would have to go into space, to another world. She would have to do something...but what? She hadn't the foggiest notion about any of it. All she knew was it involved this *p'quas'tka* psychic power, this empathy she was saddled with before she was even hatched. That got her in trouble *so* many times in the crèche, labeled her as a freak when all she did was reveal her ability to predict how others felt. She had no love for her empathic 'gift', a gift she would have been better off without.

The bell tolled four times. The line moved forward.

And there was that *alien*, that J J Ballas. The thought of him made her *r'vebbe*. Creatures with *such* power...no wonder the Ki-Elder, her sire, worried about him. What could he *possibly* want with her? She cursed him mentally, using every foul term she picked up on the streets to vent her angst, not caring if he heard her thoughts or not.

The bell tolled four times. The line moved forward.

What to do? Take the safe, predictable path which led to a life of misery, or take a desperate gamble on the unknown in hope of a better future? It wasn't long before the Justice concluded another case, then called out her name. Time for sentencing; fate had arrived. R'nemReth reluctantly stepped up to the desk with her Council.

The Justice sorted through his papers, then looked up at her. "Having heard the evidence and reviewed the Panel's finding, and in light of the petition of Civil Council, this Forum has no alternative but to sentence you to life imprisonment." R'nemReth cringed.

"What about our petition, Justice?" her Council asked. "She is awfully young to be sent to a penal nest."

The Justice paused and considered him. "She may be young, but she's no hatchling. She has proven capable of taking care of herself; the problem this Forum must deal with is *how* she does so. I'm afraid her petition is inadmissible since the only alternative is to release her back onto the streets to continue her criminal ways." He turned to R'nemReth. "You may think this harsh, but you are an habitual danger to the public peace, so there is no practical alternative." He reached for the lanyard to the Judgement Bell.

"The Forum remands you for immediate transfer to an appropriate Penal Nest for the remainder of your life. If there are no other matters to this proceeding..."

C'traBenla spoke up. "If it please, Justice, we wish to offer a petition."

The lanyard slipped from his hand. "Step forward and be heard."

She stood and nudged the mal sitting next to her. "Go on, I'ei," she muttered. He stood reluctantly, and the Warden let them through the gate to stand before the Forum.

"Who are you, sir?"

The mal beside her spoke up reluctantly. "I am Ki-Elder I'eiBida, Fleet First of the 'Dark Grays', Justice."

The Justice eyed them both dubiously. "And how may this Forum serve you, sir?"

"We...ah...we request the prisoner be transferred to us for disposal of sentence."

"Us?"

"The 'Dark Grays'."

"You propose to take her as a recruit? I know the fleet needs new tails, but you can't be this desperate!"

"No, Justice, not as a recruit; as a civilian consultant."

The Justice pondered them severely. "I don't understand. What good can she be for you?"

"She...ah...she was exposed to the Dreamsingers' powers back when the humans attacked d'enchia. Her abnormally high empathic skills resulted. We need those skills."

The Justice pondered that, and R'nemReth could sense his uncertainty. "This is most irregular," he said at last. "This Forum cannot sentence someone off-world. I'm not sure its even legal."

"I know this is extraordinary, Justice, but she can perform a needed and useful service to the nest. We need her, and it may give her a chance to earn redemption."

The Justice brooded over this, and R'nemReth clearly read the suspicion in his aura. "She is *M'mendoch,* convicted of fraud," he said at last. "She would offer herself to impressionable mals who expected her to, ah..."

21

"We read the reports, Justice," I'eiBida said, grimly.

"Indeed?" The Justice gave them a jaundiced look, but didn't make anything of it. "In any case, having received payment for her 'services', she would then disappear." There was a brief silence, as if the Justice was waiting for them to speak. Finally he added, "I *suppose* she might have done this with members of the Service?"

I'eiBida was quick on the uptake. "I wouldn't be surprised, Justice. You know how Service members can be on release pass."

"No doubt." He gave the two a stern look, and R'nemReth could tell he was looking for an excuse to be rid of an uncomfortable situation. "Can you swear to this Forum that she has in fact done this?"

I'eiBida spoke carefully. "I can swear that such incidents happen all the time, and that she no doubt was one of those involved."

The Justice pondered for a bit longer, and she could tell he was mulling over the prospect of not having to sentence a juvenile to life imprisonment. I'eiBida's statement wasn't exactly a legitimate answer. He would be taking a chance: if anyone thought to challenge his ruling, it would look bad for his judicial discretion. Against which, to sentence a juvenile fem to life in a penal nest... He made up his mind and reached for the Judgement Bell. "Very well. Since it appears she may have defrauded Service personnel, among others, this Forum will defer to the 'Dark Grays' for sentencing."

The four strokes of the bell sealed her fate.

§

The block Warden escorted her back to detention, and shortly thereafter delivered her to the interview cell where I'eiBida and C'traBenla were waiting. By time she arrived, her mind was boiling with confusion and curiosity.

"The humans *attacked* us?" she greeted them. "When did this happen?"

"I was carrying you at the time," C'traBenla said. "J J gave us and the humans psychic powers to make it easier for them to communicate with us. It brought the Contact Crisis to the breaking point, and there was a brief battle in orbit." I'eiBida's ears folded back in embarrassment and his aura turned dark. "He had to take the powers back," C'traBenla went on. "But you were affected while you were still in the egg."

Curiosity satisfied, she dismissed that as unimportant to her present fix. "So what happens now?"

"It will take a few days to crank through the paperwork," I'eiBida said. She could sense he was still unconvinced and did not approve of her. "Once that's ready, you will be transferred to our custody." He turned to C'traBenla. "I have to get to work." He left abruptly without a backward glance.

C'traBenla lagged behind after he left. "This is your chance to save yourself, R'nemReth. It won't be easy, but you can do it. Have faith in yourself."

"He doesn't much like me, does he?"

Her ears reclined in dismay. "He doesn't approve of my meddling. It's not you, it's...the circumstances. He'll come around, in time."

Privately she knew better. He was a high-achiever, a life-long Defender of the Nest with a distinguished record; her life was a sorry spectacle by comparison. It was no wonder he was embarrassed by their connection. She needed his support if she was ever to earn a Writ of Forbearance, but that would be an uphill fight against his very real disappointment. Plus what she had to do to earn that Writ was still unknown, and the prospects were not comforting. Her world being what it was, she knew the price would be high.

"Well...thank you for trying, anyway," she said at last.

*****

"A Fresh Start, Maybe"

In a life full of regrets, her new status as a 'civilian consultant' was nothing new or different, even if it was a change from life on the streets. She never did have many options in the past, usually none of them good, and now it was the same sad song, just more drawn out.

She found herself tossed tail first into a life of regimen and discipline, procedure and rules under the heel of the 'Dark Grays'. She soon learned she was far back at the uttermost back of the herd, which only made it worse. She found few sympathizers among the disciplined military, who were all too inclined to snub her or treat her with contempt. The one thing which kept them at bay was the personal endorsement and top priority from the Fleet First, and the rumors about her being his hatchling.

They treated her carefully because of it, which didn't make the experience any less unpleasant. She was kept in the lockup at the 'Dark Grays' spaceport base and escorted to and from daily sessions by two Service Wardens. They were fairly easy to get along with after her experience in the local lockups, but they were all business. She was still a convicted felon sentenced to penal exile, and they knew exactly how to insure she didn't stray. The younger one was a bright and eager rulebook *t'pithm'ig*, but the older was more mellow. He damped down his overeager partner, and went so far as to buy her a bowl of *l'ni'ddi* on occasion. It was one of the few bright spots in her loneliness, and she appreciated the gesture even if they were the Law.

They galloped her through the training program for interstellar passengers, and brief as it was, it was not pleasant. The medical regimen they inflicted on her was nasty and unnerving as they pried into her health and purged her of any infectious diseases. They weren't happy about her physical state: life on the street left its marks. From remarks she overheard, they would normally have rejected her for off-world travel, but since she came with first finger priority, they focussed on patching her together well enough to make the journey. That worried her in particular, since she had long accepted her various aches and pains as part of her lot in life.

What were they so concerned about? Fretting over their mysterious comments soon had her in a fit of *r'vebbe*.

They delivered her into the tender mercies of a physical therapist who put her through a relentless program to boost her strength and agility. The stretching exercises left her aching, and the long distance running left her winded and footsore, but over the next several hand of days her aches lessened and her endurance improved. Before she knew it, she was beginning to feel good about herself.

There were also several days spent in orbit learning how to function in zero-G. That was bad enough, but while floating around in the training module she was introduced to Zero-G 'endurance rations', which were unspeakably vile. One of her instructors commented, "The 'endurance' refers to how long you can survive eating them!" She believed it.

She also went under the microscope with a psychiatrist, who plainly wasn't thrilled by her. "Space travel is hazardous," he told her, bluntly. "You are seriously maladjusted, which puts you in real danger. Your first instinct in any crisis has to be to follow the herd, and if you go flouting the rules and slacking off, you could be killed."

She'd dealt with these *un'tdar* brain mechanics before, but this was out of her experience. She could tell he wasn't trying to 'help her' or 'cure her' so much as insure she held together and completed the mission. She never was the introspective sort, but she saw this as a telling view into the get-it-done military mindset.

She half expected him to brief her on what this 'mission' was about since he dealt with psychic matters, but he gave her nothing. In fact no one told her anything; she got the impression they didn't know. All she had to go on was it involved space travel and her overblown empathy—plus the Dreamsingers, who seemed to be calling the tune. It wasn't comforting.

Mysteries aside, they put far too much emphasis on what to do in an emergency for her peace of mind, but what really worried her was the complete lack of what to do if the ship was wrecked. It seemed if they were stranded in space by some misfortune, rescue was unlikely at best.

She stuck with it grimly despite her aches and pains and misgivings since it was her one alternative to life in a penal nest. But she hated every moment of it, and cursed the Fleet First and his priceless 'Dark Grays', condemning them all to the Uttermost Darkness with the bitterest language she could muster. Still, bad as it was, this *p'quas'tka* offered at least the *hope* of a better future.

§

Finally, after the twenty day course was finished, her Service Warden escorts delivered her to the spaceport for her journey. The boarding area was a cavernous room blocked off from the civilian airport by a fence. The room was bare and uninviting, with a plain concrete floor, light fixtures suspended from naked trusswork, and the inevitable coat of Depressing Institutional Pale Green paint. It bore the timeless, somehow weary look of all military installations.

They weren't alone. There were several hand's worth of Ic'nichi passengers, and several more hand's worth of humans, all more or less sticking with their own in two separate herds. This was the first time R'nemReth met humans up close, and after her experience with J J Ballas she was decidedly skittish about them. She tried to blend into the Ic'nichi herd followed by her two escorts who made her feel like a spotlight was focussed on her, and kept a wary eye on the aliens across the room.

Surprisingly, C'traBenla was there. "Hello R'nemReth! It's good to see you again, especially since it's not like last time."

"As if this is any better," she grumbled. "They're knotting my tail big time."

C'traBenla gave her a severe look. "Nothing is free in this Universe, youngling. You've been given a chance to earn a fresh start, but you'll have to work for it. Trust me: I know."

"I don't even know what they expect from me!"

"They haven't explained it to you?" She seemed surprised, although R'nemReth suspected otherwise. "Well, I'm sure they'll fill you in on the details in due time."

"Wonderful. I'm expected to gallop off to the ends of the Universe without a clue. What else can go wrong?"

"I do have a bit of good news for you. You are booked on ship 200, so you won't have to worry about zero-G."

"Isn't he going to see me off?" she asked, pointedly.

C'traBenla offered an embarrassed ear twitch. "No. He is very busy."

She made a contemptuous snort. "He doesn't approve of me, does he?"

"Well...no. He doesn't." She could sense C'traBenla was embarrassed. "You need to understand, he is very much a creature of duty. His whole career is dedicated to serving the nest, and he feels...uncomfortable...around you."

"Uncomfortable?" She greeted that with an angry ear twitch. "You mean he's ashamed of me!"

"You couldn't help how things turned out. You were exposed to the Dreamsingers' powers, and they altered your mind so you can't fit into the herd. It's not your fault."

They were interrupted by a youthful mal in 'Dark Grays' uniform. He was average length, wiry, with arresting green eyes. "I beg your pardon." Offered a courteous ear twitch. "Are you C'traBenla?"

"That's right," she said, coolly. "Who are you?"

"I am Second Degree Elder K'nidMin. I was assigned to escort a certain R'nemReth to her destination. I was told you could connect me with her."

"That's me," R'nemReth told him.

He offered a reassuring smile and ear twitch, although she could sense his uneasiness. What did *he* have to worry about? "Excellent! Do you have your gear?"

"It's being loaded on the shuttle." Before leaving for the spaceport she was issued military fatigues, heavy duty foot socks, an overtunic and personal gear stuffed into a bulky straddle pack.

"Then we're all set to go." They were distracted by an announcement for the next shuttle. "That's us," K'nidMin said.

"You will take good care of her, won't you?" C'traBenla asked, plaintively.

"I certainly will. The Fleet First made me *personally* responsible for her safety."

"So will I." The set of her ears was intimidating.

§

27

The ride up into orbit was rough, even if she had experienced it a few times already. These shuttles were *supposed* to be safe, but she held little confidence in something this Ancestorlessly complex wielding such enormous power. She especially hated how the acceleration crushed her into her crash cushion followed by the abrupt engine shutdown and zero-G, which left her innards bouncing around inside her.

Despite her misgivings, they made it. Once her stomach settled, she unfastened her restraint, largely because she wasn't supposed to, and plastered herself to one of the viewports for a look at their ship.

Ship 200 was the newest, grandest passenger liner in the service, built specifically for the d'enchia-earth trade and fitted for passengers of both races. It was also a radical new design, with the control module at the front and the reactor and engines way back at the rear. The habitat was built as a ring mounted amidships like a wheel on an axle. The ring rotated slowly, giving a half-gravity of centrifugal weight.

"It's *huge!*" R'nemReth was awe-struck by the sheer size of it, enough so that her troubles were temporarily brushed aside.

"It's the largest ship in our fleet," K'nidMin said as he joined her. "You can be thankful we were able to book passage. The diplomatic courier is nowhere near as comfortable."

§

Docking was routine. They squeezed through the top hatch into the central column, then took one of the elevators up to the habitat where they were greeted by the ship's Warden and the chief Steward. After giving them their room assignments, the Warden sized her up with a jaundiced look. "She's rather young to be in the 'Dark Grays', isn't she?"

"She's a civilian consultant on a special assignment," K'nidMin said. "Don't let her age fool you; she's more capable than she seems."

"And I'm no hatchling," she growled at him. "I can look after myself, thank you!"

The Warden was not convinced. "So why does she get an escort from the 'Dark Grays', then?"

28

"She's a tail-shaker. She's the Ki-Elder's hatchling."

"Ancestors! *Another* one?" The chief Steward was visibly alarmed. "Don't we have enough problems?"

"We only just got this ship back in commission!" the Warden added.

"Oh, come on," K'nidMin grumbled. "It can't be that bad!"

The Warden gave him a jaundiced look. "You weren't here, were you? It took us over a year to repair the damages."

"Really?" K'nidMin made a surprised ear twitch. "I heard the trip was difficult, but I had no idea."

The two exchanged alarmed glances. "Just pray to your Ancestors you never find out for yourself!" the Steward said.

§

"What did he mean by another one?" she asked as they headed for her cabin.

K'nidMin considered her for a long moment before answering. "You have a fellow hatching, what the humans call a 'brother'. He was a 'Dark Grays' trainee on his apprentice cruise aboard this ship. His cruise was, shall we say, *historic*."

"And it took a year to repair the damage? It must have been!"

K'nidMin offered an amused ear twitch. "It was. He not only short-circuited a possible war with the humans, but he saved a primitive race from extinction, too."

"Really? I hope to meet him some day. He sounds like fun."

§

At least ship 200 was comfortable. Her single cabin was a bit over a length square, with a fold-down bed and a chest of drawers for her newly issued clothing and personal items. It was compact, but far better than most of the places she'd slept in her years on the street.

She snooped around the public spaces and found the sanitary facilities clustered in the center of the cabin block next to one of the lounges. The lounge itself was tastefully decorated with pattern carpet, soft pastels, and light panels. The space was filled with potted plants and both human and Ic'nichi furnishings.

It was also filled with humans in addition to the Ic'nichi passengers. There were several hand of them, most either chatting

29

among themselves in their strange moaning language or going through paperwork. Two of them sat at a table playing a game which involved moving pieces one at a time around a square board.

Being so close to all those aliens made her nervous. She tried not to show her discomfort as she rubbed elbows with passing strangers, a few of whom offered a polite word or two which she couldn't understand before moving on. She felt decidedly out of place. These weren't even her kind, and they came from a culture she knew little about other than the dark rumors she'd heard over the years. The sounds were odd, the smells were odd, and they gave off an aura of vague menace which she couldn't help reacting to.

Part of both walls were large windows from which she could stare down at d'enchia passing below, which she found more comfortable than staring at all the aliens. K'nidMin found her there some time later, bemused by the sight. "It's beautiful, isn't it?"

That dragged her back to the here-and-now, and a ship filled with humans. "Are we safe with *them* here?" she asked in a nervous whisper.

He made an amused ear twitch. "Relax. These are mainly diplomatic and trade representatives, negotiation specialists, news media, and some family members." He gave her a wry smile. "*Most* of them are harmless."

"I've...never been close to them like this before."

"Best get used to it. The ship is fully booked, and nearly half the passengers are humans. They're not a bad sort, really, if you allow for them being mentally unstable."

That was not comforting. "Wonderful," she grumbled. "We're stampeding to the far end of the Universe in a ship loaded with *er'trxxda* aliens to do I have no idea what, with no idea how to do it."

He chuckled at her discomfiture. "Yes. Isn't it exciting?" It seemed this K'nidMin had a wry sense of humor. "So, have you been to late-meal yet?"

She sensed an invitation in the way he watched her, which made her nervous. "I'm not hungry. I may get something later."

He offered a dismissive ear twitch. "Late-meal usually runs for some time, but you don't want to dawdle. You may wind up going without." Before he left, he added, "I understand we'll be getting under way shortly. We need to meet later to discuss the mission."

§

They met in K'nidMin's cabin after the cafeteria shut down when the ship was already well on its way out-system. Meeting like this worried her since she figured he was planning to take advantage of her, but he was all business.

"I am a First Contact specialist, part of a small herd of experts in dealing with newly contacted races," he explained. "Unfortunately, we had a contact go bad, and we're trying to pick up the pieces, which is why we need you."

"Me? I don't know anything about contacting races! What good can I do?" This revealed what the hysteria was all about, but she still couldn't see where she fit into their schemes.

The set of his ears suggested he was unhappy with the situation. "There's a problem. The humans are involved, and they're a herd of trigger-happy *n'bna'nmn*. They made the original contact, but the natives must have mistaken them for mere animals. One of them was killed and eaten. The others fought back, killing three of the natives. Needless to say, relations with them are nonexistent at this time."

"The *humans?*" That was disturbing. She heard stories about the humans, and wasn't thrilled by the thought of adding that complication to her life. "So where do I come into this?"

K'nidMin paused to size her up, which made her uncomfortable. "The Dreamsingers can gift us with psychic powers, but our minds are not equipped to deal with them. We contact specialists received limited empathic abilities, roughly comparable to yours, but it's all we can handle, and honestly, it's a challenge at times. You already have enhanced empathy due to your exposure to the Dreamsingers while still in the egg. We hope you can connect with the aliens better than we can."

Great. This wasn't what she was expecting, which threw her a bit off balance. She could tell he was holding something back, and since it involved that big black appearing-disappearing fellow, this

31

mystery was not to be taken lightly. "Just how many aliens are there out here anyway?" she demanded.

K'nidMin cocked a bemused ear at her. "Best estimates, ten thousand or more races in this galaxy alone. As for the immediate matter, aside from us there are four: the humans, the Dreamsingers, the Li-qua and the Flyers.

"Flyers?"

"The aliens we need to contact. They are flying creatures; magnificent, really. You should see them soaring on the thermals in their mountain passes."

He opened his briefcase and handed her a large photograph. It was a long range telephoto of a huge winged creature soaring at height. The thing was pretty much all wing, broad and deep, with a horned head in front and legs tucked up underneath being the only distractions. "How...big are these creatures?" She studied the photo trying to estimate their size.

"Typical wingspan is about twenty lengths."

Twenty lengths? These things were *Ancestorlessly* huge! What really worried her was the size of those claws and the mouth full of teeth, visible even in this distant shot. They could easily carry her away. "You expect me to go up against *that?*"

"Not 'against'. We're trying to contact them, remember. All you need to do is make a connection."

She began to see why they kept her in the dark until now: it was too late to back out. She pondered the photo uneasily as he watched her all the while. She couldn't help but notice, and his attention made her nervous. Why was he so fixated on her?

Back to the photo. One obvious question came to mind. "How do you know they're intelligent? Do they have cities and stuff?"

K'nidMin seemed embarrassed. "You've touched on one of our real weaknesses. We've scanned the entire planet, and there is no sign of technology. No cities, no roads, nothing."

"They wouldn't need roads if they can fly."

K'nidMin offered a bemused ear twitch. "Good point. The fact remains we've seen no hint of technology. All the usual markers are absent, and without them we're clueless. The only reason we know they're intelligent is because the Dreamsingers told us."

That brought on a shudder. "Them. I only met one, and they're *l'cc'vn* strange. What is it with them?"

"They are the inhabitants of a gas giant world. They use psychic powers like we do speech and hands. That image you saw...what did it look like?"

"A human...big, black...he had a strange aura about him, like he could broadcast his emotions."

K'nidMin nodded. "J J Ballas. He's the only one of them we've ever seen. The person you 'saw' was actually an image projected into your mind through telepathy."

That explained how he could pop in and out. "So what do they want with us?"

"As near as we and the humans can figure, they look on us as something surpassing strange: beings without psychic powers. It seems we're objects of pity to them. In any case, we saved them from being exterminated back during the Contact Crisis. They seem to feel they owe us."

"I would think so!"

"The Dreamsingers were instrumental in setting up the joint Contact Herd. They gifted us and our human counterparts with empathy, which is all we can handle. However, since you were hatched with this ability, our hope is that you can do more than we can. I understand J J thinks so. If you can, we can contact the Flyers and resolve the problem."

That scared her. "What if I can't? I could get eaten!"

He made a placating gesture. "We'll move carefully. You'll be protected at all times."

Something C'traBenla said filtered through her rising panic: *'Nothing is free in this Universe, youngling.'* But she never expected her freedom to be so expensive!

"N-no...I can't...I-I'm scared..."

K'nidMin took her hand and gazed into her eyes. "We'll watch over you. J J knows what he's doing, and we'll be alert for any danger."

"This is *er'trxxda!*" In the back of her mind, her survival instinct was warning her of something not right. Why should her empathy be any better than theirs? It didn't add up.

"This is important, R'nemReth. This is your chance to do something huge, your chance to make a difference. We need you."

She fought down her panic as best she could. She could tell he was withholding something, but what? Her well-honed survival instinct was sounding alarms. But she was cornered, and the only thing she could do was hang on and try to keep ahead of events. *'Nothing is free in this Universe, youngling.'*

It was all too much for her overloaded spirit. There were too many aliens, too much weird *ui'DmukNa* flying around, not the least of which she was on a *starship* headed Ancestors knew where because her *mind* was altered by an alien before she was even hatched. "This is one *l'cc'vn* mess!" she muttered. "It makes my head hurt just thinking about it."

"You've had a long day, so you should get some rest. I'll meet you for first-meal in the morning." He gave her a sardonic ear twitch as she turned to leave. "And, no, I have no intention of taking advantage of you."

She left him on that note, which struck her as both ominous and mysterious. It wasn't until some time later, when she was trying to relax in the lounge with her second bowl of *'sti'eit*, that she remembered what he told her about the Dreamsingers: *'We contact specialists received limited empathic abilities...'* He was an empath. No wonder he kept staring at her: he was reading her emotions.

*****

"A First Taste Of Adventure"

Ten days later, the ship downjumped on the edge of a remote star system a dismayingly long way from anywhere. R'nemReth ignored the others crowding around her and glued herself to the lounge window for her first sight of an alien world. The sky around them was dusted with stars, so many that the blackness was tinted gray; a refreshing sight after ten days of staring at the nothingness of hyperspace. The planet's star was a blindingly bright speck ahead, the crown jewel of a vast, majestic vision which filled her with awe.

"So what do you think?" K'nidMin said as he joined her at the window. "A lovely sight, isn't it?" He gestured at their destination, which was close enough to see detail clearly. The fourth planet was a lovely blue and green world with white clouds swirling across its face and part of it hidden in its nighttime shadow. The sight filled her with foreboding about what lay ahead. When she didn't answer, he added, "This is Checkpoint, a world right on the border between us and human space."

"This is where you want me to do your thing?"

"No. This is a transit point. Ships stop here for customs before entering foreign space, but it also serves as a center for operations in this area. We will transfer to a human patrol ship headed for our destination." He studied the planet ahead. "Hmmm, no sign of them. We'll be here for a while, so we might as well go down and see what we can find out."

"What about that?" She gestured at a ship in orbit, attended by an inflatable fuel bowser and a couple small orbital tugs.

"That is ship 92, an old colony transport hulk. It served as Checkpoint for a number of years before we came here. Now it serves as an orbital platform. They don't go out any more. I doubt if they're even space-worthy."

She dismissed it as a minor detail, and returned to staring at the planet. The seas were deep blue and the land masses mottled brown and green. There were dirty white ice caps, and a thin haze of atmosphere blurred the horizon. It was strangely beautiful, strangely appealing despite her apprehension.

After ten days she was starting to feel comfortable with K'nidMin, enough so that she could open up to him a bit. "What's it like down there?" she asked, plaintively. "I've never seen another world before."

He offered her a reassuring ear twitch. "It's nice. Good climate, a bit warm being in the tropics, but lovely scenery. You'll like the natives, too."

"Natives?" That sounded ominous.

"Yes, the Li-qua."

The name was vaguely familiar. "Wasn't there something about them in the media recently?"

"Yes. They were transplanted here by a joint effort of ourselves and the humans. All the talk last year about a war with the humans was over this world. We gave it to the Li-qua instead."

She vaguely recalled hearing about a possible war, not that she paid much attention to the news since there were more pressing needs on the street. The sight of the planet ahead opened up a whole new perspective on the Universe, which roused her curiosity. "So why bring them here? Where is their home world?"

K'nidMin gave her a somber look, and his aura turned chill. "Their original world was destroyed. The two thousand-odd down there are all that are left."

The thought sent a chill through her. "That's...horrible..." All of a sudden the planet ahead wasn't so beautiful, space nowhere near so grand and majestic.

He nodded, and his aura was somber. "It is. This has been our herd's greatest priority for some time now. Part of why I was on d'enchia was to press for more assets, not only for here, but for the Flyers project as well."

"Did you have much luck with that?"

He gave her a speculative ear twitch. "Well, we got you; something I hadn't expected. I daresay you could count as 'luck'."

"It depends on your point of view," she mumbled. She understood how important this was, and was beginning to understand the essential role K'nidMin and his herd played. What she still couldn't see was what part she would have in it.

§

The next day ship 200 arrived in orbit. A shuttle was dispatched carrying seven people—the two of them plus others bound for the settlement here—along with several tons of cargo. The ride down was bumpy but routine, and ended with a vertical landing on a prefabricated metal landing pad some distance from a clutter of temporary buildings and tents.

"Thankfully *that's* over," she grumbled as they sorted themselves out. "I'm beginning to *hate* space travel." Actually travel in an interstellar liner was quite pleasant despite all the humans aboard; landing in the shuttle was another matter.

K'nidMin offered an encouraging ear twitch. "It's not so bad, really. You'll get used to it."

"That's what worries me." She hefted her straddle pack, turned toward the encampment...and came up short. There was an enormous crustacean not ten lengths away crawling toward them on four walking legs while two nasty-looking claws reached out to them. "*What is that?*" she cried in panic.

"Relax. That's our host." K'nidMin stepped between her and the creature. "Greetings, Loo-loo-ba. It is good to see you again."

"My hut is empty," the creature said in a raspy voice.

"As is mine, my friend. I bring you a gift." K'nidMin opened a package he was carrying and showed it to the creature. Inside were several odd pieces of brightly colored plastic.

"You bring colors!" The creature's aura bubbled with excitement like a hatchling with a shiny new toy. "You bring green?"

"Plenty of green, Loo-loo-ba." He glanced at R'nemReth. "I have a friend who runs a shop making plastic display cases. The Li-qua love these brightly colored scraps, so I bring some whenever I can."

"Wonderful." She edged back toward the shuttle hatch. Her hearts were racing, and she trembled in fear after that unexpected shock. So these were the natives? The humans were bad enough; she never imagined something so strange or terrifying. It was hard to believe she could ever like something so *unnatural*.

The creature sorted through the colorful scraps for a bit, then turned his eye stalks on her. "New person come?"

"Yes, Loo-loo-ba.   This is R'nemReth.   She is joining our contact herd."

"You take mate? You have young soon?"

K'nidMin laughed at her dismay. "No, Loo-loo-ba, she is not my mate.   She will work with us."   R'nemReth blushed in embarrassment.

The creature, Loo-loo-ba, examined her with both eye stalks. "My hut is empty," he said.   "K'nidMin take mate, have young. This good."

K'nidMin laughed, and threw a speculative glance her way. "All in good time, my friend. All in good time."

§

"Your *mate?*" she hissed at him as they headed for the office grotto. "What kind of ideas have you been feeding them?"

"Relax. They come from a simple culture where finding mates is a lot less involved than it is in ours."   He was silent for a moment, and R'nemReth could sense him brooding. "Plus finding mates and expanding their population is all that matters to them right now.   A large part of the effort here has been helping to selectively pair them to insure against inbreeding. You could say they're fixated on it."

That made sense under the circumstances, not that she wanted to dwell on it. "What did...he...mean by his hut is empty?"

"He was offering us his acceptance as their Wise One, their leader. It's an ancient tradition among them."

"By offering us his hut?"

"That is just symbolic, actually.   He was accepting you into their species. It's not something done readily, but you come highly recommended."

She was getting past her original shock, and the notion of being 'accepted' into their species bemused her.   "He seems rather hatchling-like. Are they *hro'n'nad?*"

"Hardly!   They are far more intelligent than us.   We are still trying to understand how their minds work, in fact." He glanced at her. "There's another area where you could be a big help."

The weather was too warm for her comfort, and the strong daylight beating down on them soon had her overheated.   "Is it

38

always like this?" she grumbled. "I swear I'm going to fall asleep out here."

"The days are a bit much," K'NidMin said. "You'll want to switch to tropical kit. The nights are mild, anyway."

"Ancestors, I *hope* so," she griped.

§

They were assigned to temporary quarters which turned out to be a newly erected tent at the end of a row along the beach. "There's a chronic shortage of space with all the Learnéds, media types and ground support stampeding in here." K'nidMin gestured at a row of metal buildings going up nearby. "These will be adequate for the few days we'll be here."

At least the tent was roomy and well equipped. Inside was a folding bed, a folding table and a pair of collapsable seat cushions. A solar powered lamp hung from the center peak, with its power panel on the tent top above. There was a heavy waterproof ground cover, and one side wall was raised and tied off, providing a cool breeze and a view of the sea.

"This will do, I guess," she said, dismissively. The canvas kept the strong daylight at bay, so it was fairly comfortable inside. She tossed her straddle pack on the bed and dug through it for a few personal items. "What about the restroom? Where do I go to get a shower?"

He settled on one of the seat cushions and gestured down the line of tents. "At the head of this row, down near the beach. There's no hot water, but we hardly miss it in this climate."

That figured. She was well used to ad-hoc personal care, not always easy to find on the street. She dug into her straddle pack and came up with a set of tropical fatigues, then puttered around impatiently while waiting for him to leave. Instead he remained seated, annoying her with a steady stream of small-talk until he was starting to get on her nerves. Finally she gave him a sharp look. "There's only one bed in here."

He shook out of his bemused state. "Oh. Sorry. My tent is next door." He gathered up his straddle pack and beat a hasty retreat, trailed by an aura of resentment.

§

K'nidMin insisted they return to her tent after late-meal, saying it was time to get down to business. R'nemReth was uneasy, wondering what he had in mind as he closed the open tent side and lit the lamp. "The time has come to start prepping you for the mission," he said as he settled on one of the camp stools. His aura was concerned and a bit uneasy, which put her nerves on edge.

"Prepping me? How?"

K'nidMin considered her for a long moment before he answered, and his hesitation did nothing for her composure. "You were chosen for this mission because you were exposed to the Dreamsingers' power while still in the egg," he said at last. "From what I was told, it will give you the ability to absorb further psychic powers, more than the rest of us can handle. We need to do it now so you will have time to adjust before we reach our destination."

She was suddenly afraid. "What do you mean 'further powers'? What do you have in mind?"

"We need a telepath to contact the Flyers." He was trying hard to explain without panicking her. "J J can give you that ability."

She knew all along the moment when she had to perform would come, and managed to put off thinking about it until now, but this was an ugly, unexpected twist. "This isn't fair! No one told me about this!"

"I know. I'm sorry..."

"Sorry? You ambushed me!"

K'nidMin's aura was hot with embarrassment. "It isn't fair, I know. But you'll need this ability."

"Well I won't do it! No one asked me if I would agree to this! I was tossed into this tail-first, and now you want some alien *riv'Agna* to alter my mind!"

"I'm on your side, R'nemReth; honest. You were given a *p'quas'tka* deal from the very start, and I *sincerely* want to see you get through this and earn that Writ of Forbearance." He offered an earnest ear twitch and his aura was full of concern. "I've been gifted with empathy, so I know how strange it feels. Be brave; this is your chance to start over."

"I-I-I don't want to be brave..."

40

"Sometimes, when you're in a bad situation, the best thing is to plunge in head first and plow through it." He reached out and took her hand. "This is critical to the success of the mission, and to your future," he pleaded with her. "You can do this. You're strong, a survivor. You can make it happen and earn your second chance."

His aura of concern was sincere, and she could sense his sympathy...but there was his treachery to consider, too. Now it seemed she would have to take on more psychic powers—that this was part of the program all along. And they kept this part from her until it was too late to back out.

"You trapped me! If you think I'll trust you now, you're badly mistaken!"

"It wasn't my idea, R'nemReth, really. We should have been honest with you, but I was under orders."

"Under *orders!?* It's your *p'quas'tka* Fleet First! That *un'tdar* had it in for me from the start!"

"He...felt you...weren't able to carry through..."

"He felt? He can't feel *anything* except his duty!"

"He *is* concerned about you, R'nemReth. I felt it in him when I received my orders." He stood and took her hand in a comforting gesture. "You have to understand: being a defender is not easy. We deal with harsh realities. Sometimes we have to sacrifice lives for the greater good. It doesn't make him a *riv'Agna*. He did what he felt he had to do."

She wrenched her hand free and turned her back on him, trying to keep her tears in check. "I hate you! How would he know how I'd react? You could have told me in spite of your *l'cc'vn* orders!"

"I should have," he said, softly. "But duty is a harsh thing. You can't compromise on it; that only leaves you open to further weakness. I'll make it up to you if I can."

"Why should I trust you?"

"R'nemReth, this is more urgent than personalities, more important than you or me, or the Fleet First. We have a problem with a critical program, and you may be the one hope we have of solving it. It isn't fair for you to be tail-knotted like this, but life isn't fair. The only realistic thing for you to do is play your part, solve the problem, and earn a new life for yourself."

41

He was right: as much as she hated the idea, her only hope of a normal life was to complete this mission; and some new and unknown psychic powers were the key. The price of her second chance was appalling! She was trapped in a hopeless fix from the moment she hatched, and now her fate had come to claim her.

"I'm...scared..." She was finally able to confront her darkest feelings and reach out to someone. "Please...they're going to a-alter m-my mind..."

"I know. These psychic powers are unnatural; it's no surprise you're afraid." He took her hand again and gave her a reassuring smile. "I've dealt with the Dreamsingers before. We all have. They aren't evil. You can trust them."

She fought to damp down her fear, drawing on him for support. At least she had his sympathy, which helped a little, and he seemed to genuinely regret deceiving her. Finally she managed to nod. "I...don't have a choice...I guess..."

K'nidMin gave her a reassuring ear twitch. "I'll call him."

A moment later J J Ballas appeared right in the middle of the tent, looming over them both. "Well howdy there, Lil-Missy. It's good t' see you come this far." She cringed at his sudden appearance, and didn't answer.

"She's kind of skittish, J J." K'nidMin's voice was tight with tension. "You'll need to move slowly. There's still time before we reach the Flyers' world."

He gave K'nidMin a jaundiced look. "This-here is overdue, in fact. She'll need practice t' learn how t' control her power. You should-a done this earlier."

K'nidMin offered a rueful ear twitch; his emotions were blanketed out by J J's overwhelming presence. "I was under orders," he said, unhappily.

J J emitted an aura of disapproval. "Ah'll have a word wit' him 'bout it. But it ain't no matter now." He turned his attention to R'nemReth. "She a smart one, she can handle it. But yo' need t' give her time t' adjust, you hear?"

"All the time she needs, J J," K'nidMin promised.

She edged back against the far wall as J J focussed on her. "What are you going to do?"

"Well now, don' you worry none, Lil-Missy. Ol' J J won't do you no harm." She could feel an aura of concern radiating from him like the strong tropical daylight as he loomed over her. "All ah'm gonna do is give yo' the telepath, that's all. That way you can talk wit' folks who don't speak yo' language." He smiled at her, and his aura of calm reassurance flooded through her. "It won't hurt none. Promise."

She was far from convinced, and terrified by this *creature's* power. "I...I...never ag-greed to this!" she stammered.

"It's important, Lil-Missy. Most folks can't take these powers, but you can. Ah see it in you."

"This is key to solving the Flyer crisis," K'nidMin pleaded with her. "This is your big chance." He took both her hands and gave her a reassuring smile. "Be strong, R'nemReth, you can do it."

"An' I'll be watching over you, Lil-Missy. Ol' J J won't let you come t' no harm."

She struggled to get her terror under control, which took some doing, and cursed the ill-luck of her hatching. But it was too late for regrets now. As terrified as she was at what they planned, it had to be done if she was ever going to have a normal life. "This...isn't...fair..."

"Life ain't fair, Lil-Missy, but don' you worry about them powers none. Ol' J J will protect you."

"This is your chance to escape your past," K'nidMin added. "Be strong, R'nemReth."

Finally, her hearts racing and limbs trembling, she managed to damp down her fear enough to go on. She took several deep breaths to steady herself. "I...I'm...ready..."

She heard J J's voice in her mind. *'All rightie.'* Then she felt the *oddest* sensation deep in her head; the scene faded for a moment, then she cringed as a flood of faint voices came pouring into her mind, staggering her. The enclosed tent seemed to stretch to infinity, a confusing vastness full of whispered thoughts and emotions which left her dazed and disoriented.

The next thing she knew, K'nidMin held her by one arm, steadying her. *'Are you alright?'* It took her a moment to realize it was his thought, not spoken words.

"There's...s-so much n-noise..." she gasped as she reeled under the deluge of thoughts. "Can't...too much..."

'You'll be a mite confused at first,' J J's thought came to her. *'Thas why this should-a been done on the ship. It'll take a bit of gettin' used to with all this-here noise. You best lay down an' rest fo' a while. It'll pass in time.'* She looked around in near panic, but J J was gone.

K'nidMin guided her to the bed. "Get some rest," he said. "I'll look after you."

"Y-you got me into this!" she sobbed. "Why should I trust you?"

She could feel his resentment even through the psychic storm. "I'm trying to help, R'nemReth. Get some rest." He left abruptly.

*****

"The Price Of Hope"

Evening settled as she lay staring at the tent wall. The temperature dropped as the light faded, and a cool breeze came in through the open doorway. There was a faint smell of a camp fire, and someone was playing an instrument and singing in the distance. She ignored it all and lay in the dark, trying to contain the endless flood of thought and emotion pouring through her mind from everyone in the area. How many hundreds? Thousands? She was overwhelmed by the psychic white noise, like countless whispered conversations too faint to read but too strong to ignore.

The psychic storm gradually faded as people turned in for the night. The vast multitude didn't die away completely, but the remaining voices were faintly distinguishable, the pressure bearable. She lay huddled under a blanket, hiding in the dark from herself, thankful for the momentary respite, and wondered how long she could last before losing her mind completely. She bitterly cursed the Ki-Elder, her own father, for interfering in her life. He must have ordered K'nidMin to hold off until it was too late for her to back out. She swore she would give him a piece of her mind when she got back to d'enchia, if she didn't lose it first.

The evening grew late. A cool breeze came in off the water, sending the temperature down to where she was uncomfortable. She finally got up the gumption to pull the blanket over her head, and drifted off into a troubled sleep.

§

A Learnéd Z'gehRoo turned up at her tent bright and early the next morning while she was still half asleep after a restless night. "Welcome to our little herd, R'nemReth, he said with an uncomfortable smile. "I've been waiting to meet you."

"So who are you?" She tried to pick up on his thoughts, but they were lost in the general psychic blizzard.

"I am the contact herd's xenopsychologist." He was elderly, gaunt and nervous, and his utility fatigues were completely out of character for him. There was something about his nervousness which set her on edge. "K'nidMin asked me to work with you to master your telepathic ability."

She struggled to sit up. "Can you really do anything? All the voices in my head are driving me *er'trxxda.*"

He reacted with a spastic ear twitch and an aura of alarm she could feel even through the psychic storm. "I...know it is difficult. It will take time and effort, but there are ways to desensitize yourself." He made a visible effort to pull himself together, and settled on a seat cushion. "So clear your mind, focus on being calm, and let's get started, shall we?"

They spent the day with Z'gehRoo focussed on teaching her a form of human mental self-discipline called 'Zen'. As odd as it sounded, she dug into it desperately, eager to try anything which could shut off the flood of psychic noise rolling through her mind. It was hard to focus; at times the mental flood drowned out what Z'gehRoo was saying. Slowly, bit by bit, she learned how to control her constant distraction, to tamp down her awareness of the mental storm. The relentless white noise never faded completely, but by late afternoon she was able to reduce it enough so she could think rationally.

"You're doing good," Z'gehRoo said as they wrapped up a long, trying day. "You are making remarkable progress, in fact."

She was physically and mentally wrung out, and didn't feel like she accomplished anything for all their effort. "I still have this *p'quas'tka* noise in my mind," she grumbled.

"Full adjustment will take time. Nothing happens overnight in psychotherapy. Keep practicing your *mantras* and your abilities will grow in time."

"Wonderful. If I don't go *er'trxxda* first."

He twitched all over, and she felt a flush of fear from him again. "You shouldn't dwell on that," he said. "Think positive and practice your mantras."

She wondered, after he left, what he was so alarmed about.

§

The second day got off to a ragged start after another sleepless night. Learnéd Z'gehRoo spent the morning coaching her as she repeated her *mantras* again and again, trying desperately to control her thoughts and tune out the psychic background. It sounded silly, but the white noise was diminished some more by mid-day.

K'nidMin and Loo-loo-ba turned up then with something to eat. She wasn't really hungry, but seized on the break as a chance to wind down.

"How is she doing?" K'nidMin asked.

"She is improving," Z'gehRoo said after careful consideration. "Unfortunately she is too wound up and it holds her back." So much for yesterday's 'remarkable progress'. "I am confident she can stabilize her power, but it will take time."

K'nidMin offered her a reassuring smile. "You can do it," he said to her. "Just relax and focus; it'll come to you."

The two got off into a long-winded discussion of her psychic powers, ignoring her while she squatted off to one side nibbling her mid-meal and resenting their attitude. Loo-loo-ba squatted next to her, which made her uncomfortable. She always was repelled by crustaceans, and the ones on d'enchia were tiny. Loo-loo-ba was enormous: being this close to him, especially those monstrous claws, made her nervous. His presence was a constant distraction which drew her attention. As she watched him, she began to sense something. It was just a faint presence, but it shone like a bright light against the formless psychic background. Whatever it was, it appealed to her, drawing her like a flame of crystal clarity. She puzzled over it for some time before realizing she was catching his thoughts: strange, alien thoughts. She was surprised by how crisp and decisive they were, as if each was carefully put together with deep deliberation and single-minded purpose. Yet they came pouring out of him in a steady stream.

As she listened, she began to sense he was pondering several subjects at once. She was bemused to actually be hearing the thoughts of an alien, and stared at Loo-loo-ba, mesmerized, as his memories unfolded in her mind: walking along the sea bottom...feeding on tasty seaweed...the joys of mating and witnessing his latest clutch of eggs...his deep sorrow over the destruction of their home world and people...a new eye stalk sheathe woven with bits of green...his deep gratitude to the Ic'nichi and humans for giving them a second chance...it was a flood tide of clear, distinct images, as if he was carrying on several conversations at once.

47

Loo-loo-ba must have felt her mental presence. He turned and looked at her with both eye stalks. *'You be his mate?'* he asked.

She flushed with embarrassment. *'p'quas'tka I will! I can't stand him!'*

Her reaction interrupted their debate. "What is it?" K'nidMin asked.

"I...um...I was just following his thoughts." She gestured at Loo-loo-ba.

"You can read his mind?" Z'gehRoo was excited. "What is he thinking?"

"It's hard to say. He's...thinking about a lot of things...all at once. It's hard to follow."

"You shouldn't be prying like that," K'nidMin said.

'I do not mind,' Loo-loo-ba's thought came to her.

"He...he said it's alright," she mumbled in dismay. This hearing other people's thoughts so clearly was unexpected and more than a bit alarming. So this is what telepathy felt like? It left her feeling *violated* somehow.

"This is a major breakthrough!" Z'gehRoo said. "She's making more progress than I hoped. With her ability we can start really delving into the Li-qua's psychology. This could be the answer we've needed!"

"What do you mean? Answer to what?"

"We've been struggling to help the Li-qua ever since they came here," K'nidMin said. "But they are having a hard time adapting to this new world."

That surprised her. "So what's the problem? From what you told me, this place is ideal for them."

"Colonizing a new world is a lot more difficult than it seems. There are a lot of things, new predators in particular as well as local food and disease issues. The local waters are hazardous with unfamiliar predators: their youngling mortality rate is nothing short of catastrophic. Their population is dwindling as a result."

"We try to pass on the results of our research and absorb their reports of conditions out at sea, but the language barrier is holding us back." Z'gehRoo's aura was tormented. "We're losing the battle to save these people!"

She didn't like the sound of that. "So what does this mean to me? You're plotting something, aren't you?"

Z'gehRoo was so excited that he missed her foreboding tone entirely. "Your telepathy will make communications so *much* easier! It would improve our research and help the Li-qua to adapt to local conditions, which could make all the difference."

That was exactly the *wrong* thing to say just then, and it sent a shiver through her. "So get the mighty J J Ballas to give *you* telepathy, then!" she snapped at him. "I am not some lab *P'grrt'p* to use for experiments!" Z'gehRoo stared at her in wide-eyed dismay, then retreated in haste.

"Great," K'nidMin grumbled. "Now you did it."

"What?" She turned on him in annoyance. "So I hurt his feelings? Big *p'quas'tka*! I don't need some *un'tdar* brain mechanic talking down to me!"

K'nidMin gave her a sharp look, and his aura became angry. "For your information, that *un'tdar* brain mechanic *did* receive telepathy from J J. He lasted ten days, and needed nearly a year of psychiatric treatment before he could return to work!"

§

There never was much free time, but their confrontation left her at loose ends for the moment, so she went down to the beach to brood. She found a quiet spot above the surf in the shade of some tall grass, and settled in to try to put her mind at ease.

She had never seen an ocean before, and the sight bemused her. The heat of the day was passing, and people of both races were relaxing on the sand or splashing in the surf. A small herd of humans were swatting a large ball back and forth across a net, while another herd were building a camp fire. The air was tinged with wood smoke and cooking smells. It was all strangely soothing to her overburdened mind.

She was still dismayed at her telepathic ability, in particular her tuning in to Loo-loo-ba's thoughts. She could actually read the thoughts of an alien being! She never would have believed it if it hadn't happened to her. Thankfully Loo-loo-ba didn't seem to mind, which was surprisingly kind of him. She would have been freaking paranoid if it happened to her. She went over those thoughts again, savoring their crisp clarity. It was all so *alien*, yet so soothing at the same time. As she daydreamed, she began losing her fear of the armored crustaceans. They were revolting in appearance, but their minds... Their minds were something else.

And then there was Z'gehRoo's panic reaction, which alarmed her as she pondered it. She could see why he was so easily upset, and it made her worry just how far this would go. She was afraid of going *er'trxxda*, and maybe winding up in an institution herself. They were playing with something unnatural, and she was caught up right in the middle of it.

Two Li-qua came trundling up out of the surf and passed nearby with no more than a casual glance her way. Others were mingling with the humans and Ic'nichi along the beach. It was reassuring to see beings of such different species getting along in simple harmony. If only her mind could be so at peace. There were no answers, no reassurance to be found in the tranquil scene or in her mind. She felt terribly alone, like she never felt before.

There were clouds drifting in as the daylight faded and the breeze picked up. She reluctantly left the beach with its scenes of simple happiness and returned to her tent.

§

Her mental exercises with Learnéd Z'gehRoo continued the next day, even though relations between them were strained. She was embarrassed over hurting him the day before, and made a special effort to be polite and cooperative. As a result, she made real progress in her 'zen' studies.

K'nidMin and Loo-loo-ba turned up again at mid-day. "So how goes the battle?" he asked.

"She is making good progress," Z'gehRoo said.

She could sense K'nidMin was uneasy as he turned to her. "R'nemReth..." he asked, carefully. "...would you be willing to link with Loo-loo-ba again? We're having a tough time trying to communicate with the Li-qua. The project to help them get reestablished is faltering because of it."

That caught her off guard, and her first reaction was to refuse. But then, Loo-loo-ba's crisp, incisive thoughts were *such* a pleasure... "I'm...not sure what I can do," she said, uncertainly.

50

"We'll never know unless you try." He gave her a pleading look and an earnest ear twitch. "Please? Will you try? They need you."

"Well..." She turned from him to Loo-loo-ba; he was visually frightening, but the memory of his beautiful alien mind softened her unease. And they *did* ask, for once. "Um, I guess I can."

K'nidMin stepped aside, and she confronted the alien. The tent seemed to fade into the background as her consciousness moved past his surface and deep into his mind.

'...many young taken by predators...humans too noisy...' His thoughts came spilling into her like a cascade of ideas and emotions. *'...long seaweed tastes odd...the sensation of exploring an undersea trench...his present mate was a poor choice...the (untranslatable) seaweed grows poorly...much unhappiness among the females...they needed more nesting huts...the warmth of this world's daylight warming him...hungry...fearful for the eggs...can this one help?...must sharpen his claws...another mal taken by something out there...'*

She was forced to withdraw, overwhelmed. "I don't know how he does it. He just seems to carry on several lines of thought at once." She was amazed at the clarity and speed of his mind. "I can link with him, but there's so much going on in there, it's hard to sort it all out."

Z'gehRoo was bemused. "It's a shame she's not a trained psychologist. She doesn't know what to look for."

"Does anyone know what to look for?" K'nidMin said in response to her hurt expression. "You've always worked from outside; doing psychology from inside has never been tried before."

"There is that." Z'gehRoo pondered her for a long moment, and his aura was...mixed. "This offers so *many* possibilities for advancing research and treatment. If, perhaps, I could instruct her in some of the basics..."

All this talk of her, talking over and around her as if she was an inanimate object, was getting on her nerves. "Well don't count on me," she snapped. "I have no intention of wallowing through *your* thoughts!"

51

That upset him again, and after a few hasty remarks he left. "Really, R'nemReth, that was *un'brapta*," K'nidMin grumbled. "We're just trying to help."

She was in no mood to take criticism from *him,* either. "Just trying to help yourselves and your precious mission!"

"Think what you please, then!" He stomped out, leaving his familiar aura of resentment in his wake.

§

Their little blow-up netted her some more free time which she spent on the beach trying to unwind. Once her temper faded she was sorry for snapping at them. They were simply doing their jobs, and K'nidMin at least seemed to be concerned about her. These *l'cc'vn* psychic powers made a mess of everything!

A short while later Loo-loo-ba came scuttling by, and paused to speak with her. *'You help Li-qua?'* he asked, plaintively.

His simple plea hurt, especially with the danger the Li-qua faced. *'I...can't. I-I'm sorry. This is hard enough already.'*

Loo-loo-ba was silent for a moment, then thought, *'My hut is empty.'* He turned and scuttled away.

They wanted so *much* from her! Wasn't it bad enough already? It started out with the Flyers, then being saddled with these *p'quas'tka* psychic powers which threatened to drive her *er'trxxda.* Now they wanted her to work with the Li-qua and the Arbiters and the Ancestors and who knew who else. She could see it would never end. She was saddled with abilities which made her their quick and easy answer to problems which would otherwise require hard effort. It wasn't fair!

She thought about Loo-loo-ba and his beautiful, clear mind: she would love to visit his thoughts again. It was a shame what happened to them; if any race deserved to live, it was them. The more she considered it, the more she came to like that enormous crustacean. He was visually frightening, but on the inside...

For the first time in a long time, years, she felt ashamed of herself; ashamed for complaining about her own problems when the Li-qua were so much worse off. Would it be so bad to help them? There were tears on her snout. They were in desperate need, on the verge of extinction. *'You're in enough trouble already,'* she reminded herself, not that it eased her burden. Staying here to help the Li-qua could take a lifetime, a lifetime with these *p'quas'tka* psychic powers clogging up her mind. She couldn't face that, even with the pangs of guilt troubling her.

And Loo-loo-ba forgave her.

She tried to put the ugly feelings out of her mind. What would other aliens be like, she wondered? What would the Flyers' thoughts feel like? Predators? Barbaric? Soaring on the breeze? Aside from a few shuttle trips, she had never been off the ground in her life. She stared at the clouds on the horizon and imagined flapping her wings, catching the thermals as the ground wheeled far below...

It all seemed hollow somehow.

§

Evening brought a rain shower, so she turned in early. There was so much going on in her mind that she couldn't sleep, so she stared into the darkness as she listened to the rain fall. After a while she sensed K'nidMin somewhere nearby, probably in his tent. He was thinking about her, which caught her attention, so she reached out toward him out of idle curiosity, wondering what he really thought about her.

That mysterious resentment she felt earlier turned out to be his vexation at her always assuming the worst about him. That was a surprise, but she had to admit he was right. And it turned out he *was* attracted to her, which confused her since she had too many rough edges to think of herself as pretty. She dug deeper, wondering why he would be interested in her. What caught his eye was her survival instinct, her endurance and her stubborn determination—traits she never realized she had—and he sympathized with all she suffered in the past. She never thought of attractiveness in those terms before. It made her wonder what sort of image she actually presented to the world.

She lay in the dark and followed his thoughts as he daydreamed about her. They were a revelation which warmed and dismayed her at the same time. She had too many issues in his opinion...was way too defensive...he understood how she felt...helping the Li-qua was far more than she bargained for...she was afraid of her psychic powers, with good reason...she was hurt so often she didn't know how to trust anyone...she was emotionally battered...she was a survivor...one of the 'lost younglings'...still, she could offer a lot...if she would only loosen up...strong-willed and self-reliant...she would make a fine mate someday...

Embarrassed, she withdrew.

§

She was subdued the next morning, reflecting on what she learned the night before. K'nidMin shared first-meal with her, and noticed the change in her, although he didn't say anything. Truth, she was uncertain what to do. He genuinely cared about her, but she was reluctant to get involved with anyone. There was her fate back on d'enchia hanging over her, plus his life was galloping around the Universe to uncomfortable and dangerous places. But then...he cared about her...no one ever cared about her before. And he was a decent, likable sort. What to do?

She had no answer to that one, but decided she could at least quit fighting them and get with the program. The sooner she solved whatever problem they needed her for, the sooner she would have more options.

The days went by. The lessons continued. Her skills, though crude, improved steadily as she worked at her training. It wasn't long before she discovered she could receive a thought from one person and rebroadcast it to several others in real time, which stirred great excitement in K'nidMin and Z'gehRoo. "This is marvelous!" Z'gehRoo was practically dancing with joy. "This is something we never expected!"

"One which will prove invaluable, too," K'nidMin said. He was more reserved than the excitable Learnéd, but his aura flooded her with approval. "You could be a real asset to the Arbiters as well as our contact herd."

"Yes, well, don't fret about losing me to the diplomats just yet. I agreed to help you with this problem. Anything more remains to be seen."

She could sense K'nidMin was pleased by that, and by her change from flat refusal to reluctant possibility.

§

Another evening came. The weather was blustery, the wind stirring the tent canvas and causing the ropes to creak. R'nemReth turned in early and lay listening to the night and the faint stirrings which still filtered into her consciousness. She was bemused by how much progress she made in her short time here, and how seemingly natural telepathy had become. Her frantic, desperate struggles of only a few days ago seemed like distant memories. There was more to this, and to her, than she originally realized.

She listened idly to the gentle murmur of thought and emotion from those nearby, and as she did she began to understand a new truth about herself. Her long-standing instinct—her street instinct —was to grab any advantage, and now she had an advantage unique to her species. Telepathy gave her a powerful edge; what she could do with such an edge opened up all *sorts* of avenues. But how could she use this advantage? That thought, and the glittering possibilities, kept her awake, staring into the dark while her mind raced.

The gentle murmur intruded into her awareness. Curious, she reached out with her mind, sampling the thoughts and emotions of those around her. The Ic'nichi nearby were relaxing over snacks and games and conversations. There was a warm glow of togetherness, of the comforting presence of being part of the herd. She envied them, and felt like an outsider. She felt lost.

Further afield, she sensed the sharp, clear minds of the Li-qua. Loo-loo-ba's thoughts fascinated her; those of the Li-qua as a whole filled her with wonder. As she sampled here and there, she was amazed by their crystal clarity, their rapid-fire intellect, and most of all by their *alienness*. It was a refreshing new sensation in her life. Maybe exploring the Universe and meeting new species wouldn't be so bad after all? She was tempted.

She ranged further, passing over the Li-qua village to the human compound in the distance. What she found was a seething swamp of raw emotion which rocked her to her core. A burst of anger caught her attention, and she homed in on it curiously. From what she could sense, one of them was a belligerent drunk, and two others were trying to calm him down. *'Humans!'* she thought in disgust.

She swept on, but all the humans she came upon were pretty much the same: angry or depressed or scheming or cynical or envious. Like she used to be. She saw herself in the dark, and the idea of lowering herself to that level, of going back to the street in her soul, repelled her. No, she wouldn't use this gift for selfish reasons. She couldn't. She was better than this. She had to be if she was ever to be truly free. Her mind made up, she felt as if a burden was lifted from her.

Then she decided, on a daring impulse, to reach out to J J Ballas, to sample his thoughts...

'No, Lil-Missy, you ain't ready fo' that.' His unseen presence filled her with awe and foreboding. *'Likely you won't never be ready fo' that.'*

...She retreated hastily and the presence faded. Chastened for the moment, she quit dreaming about the future and went to sleep.

§

She was awakened out of an exhausted sleep by K'nidMin calling to her. She managed to open one eye and glared into the darkness. "What?" she moaned as she nervously searched the gloom of her tent. "Where are you?"

'I'm in Operations. Our ship just jumped in-system. It will be in orbit late tomorrow.'

That was a relief; she didn't need him creeping around in the dark while she was sleeping. Then she remembered they could communicate by telepathy. She'd been alarmed over nothing. She vented her upset at being awakened for such trivia, concluding with, *'What time is it, anyway?'*

'It's past midnight, local time.' She could feel a faint aura of embarrassment from somewhere across the compound. *'You were asleep, weren't you?'*

She pulled the cover up over her head. *'Brilliant! No wonder they put you in charge. I'll sleep soundly, thanks to you!'* She could sense his amusement as his presence faded.

*****

"Committed"

In a way she was sorry to leave Checkpoint, for all the drama and mental strain she went through there. That warm tropic beach was a pleasant refuge in her memory, and it wasn't long before she missed the crystal clarity of Loo-loo-ba's thoughts. But she wasn't out here for her entertainment. Now that her telepathic power was more or less under control, it was time to get to the main mission. She looked to the unknown ahead with no small amount of apprehension.

The human ship 'Comanche' offered nothing like the comforts of ship 200. The habitat was compact and cramped, and the only luxuries were a zero-G mist shower they couldn't fit into and a microwave. Sleeping accommodations for the three of them were zero-G hammocks strung in the upper cargo deck. The rest of the deck was filled with pallets of supplies restrained by heavy nets so getting sleep meant running the risk of shifting cargo. Water was rationed, so sponge bathing was limited, but at least there was an Ic'nichi zero-G toilet fitted with a privacy booth of bedsheets—a field expedient for this ship's assignment.

Meals were standard issue endurance rations. At least there was plenty of instant *V'liz*. "These things are horrible!" R'nemReth shoved her half-eaten ration back in its wrapper in disgust. After three days in space, she couldn't stomach them any more. "Can't you people do better than this?"

"Believe me, we've been complaining about these things for a century now, with no improvement." K'nidMin chomped away on his ration stoically. "You get used to it after a while."

"More like resigned to it," Learnéd Z'gehRoo muttered. "They'll keep us alive at least. Not that we'll enjoy it."

She, K'nidMin and Z'gehRoo killed time in the ship's common deck. She was learning the harsh truth of the old saying that boredom was the greatest danger in space. She was constantly ill at ease being on a human ship, and the only diversion seemed to be an endless game of something called 'poker'. At least there were just thirty-four aboard including K'nidMin, Z'gehRoo and her. The vast emptiness of hyperspace was a blessed silence.

"I hope there's real food where we're going," she grumbled. She tried to rinse the taste out of her mouth with a sip of *V'liz*, then went back to nibbling her ration. Microwaved instant *V'liz* in squeeze bottles: another burden in her litany of despair.

§

They arrived at their next destination twelve days later, somewhere deep in human space, and it proved to be a very different proposition from Checkpoint. The weather was chill and damp when they emerged from their shuttle onto another patch of pre-fab metal sheeting a fair walk from the encampment. The sky was filled with thin clouds drifting rapidly in from the sea, and there was the scent of rain in the air.

"It's *cold*," she complained as she tucked her hands into the folds of her jacket. "You picked a great time to come here."

"It's always like this." K'nidMin gestured at the scudding clouds. "This world has a cooler climate than d'enchia or Checkpoint. The planet has very little axial tilt, so it never gets really hot or cold. There isn't much snow, at least in the lower elevations, but it does rain a lot."

"Wonderful. I *hate* rain."

She paused to look out across this new world, and was not impressed. The landing pad sat on a wide, barren plain stretching inland from a rocky coast to low wooded foothills shrouded by patchy fog. A broad river emerged from a deep cut and meandered through a muddy delta to the sea. Beyond, in the distance, jagged mountains soared into a dirty sky. The plain was barren except for a carpet of low mossy growth, which was burnt away from the edges of the landing pad by repeated shuttle landings, revealing sickly brown mud.

She gestured at a herd of strange-looking animals grazing in the distance. "Are they dangerous?"

"Those? No. In fact they don't come anywhere near here. You do need to watch out for the stickly bushes, though." He gestured to a low shrub which sprouted a solid coat of thorns. "Those things are needle sharp."

"Lovely," she grumbled as she studied the landscape uneasily. "This'd make a great tourist attraction."

"Actually, you aren't entirely wrong. One of the humans, a Master Sargent MacIntosh, said this reminds him of his native Scotland."

"It does, eh? Poor *riv'Agna*."

They were interrupted by a utility vehicle driven by four humans from the encampment. The shuttle crew opening their cargo door as the vehicle pulled along side, and two humans stood guard on a light machine gun while the rest started shifting cargo.

'Aren't those two going to help?' she thought to K'nidMin.

'They need to stay alert,' K'nidMin thought back. *'Plus the humans can be uncooperative at times.'* He pondered them for a bit, and their surly mood was plain. *'They must be in a snit again. We may have some minor crisis in the camp.'*

At the rate the cargo was being transferred, they would be forever off-loading, so she and K'nidMin hefted their straddle packs and set off down the muddy track leading to the distant camp. "I feel odd," she said. "Like I could float." That worried her, and she wondered if this was an after effect of prolonged weightlessness.

"The gravity here is only eighty percent of d'enchia's," K'nidMin told her. "It helps the Flyers, and makes it easier for us to do our work."

"Oh." R'nemReth was a bit embarrassed. It appeared she had a lot to learn yet.

The camp sat on a low embankment overlooking the ocean where restless waves crashed against the rocks and filled the air with flying spray. One side of the camp was right along the edge of the high ground bordering the river delta. The encampment itself was a fortified post with a dismaying array of machine guns mounted at strategic points to cover the approaches to the camp. Everyone was armed: the humans manned the gun positions on constant alert, and even the Ic'nichi bore sidearms. Various prefab buildings were arrayed in a circle, with tall sharpened stakes ringing the camp. The central clearing was roofed with a net woven of barbed wire, with more tangles of barbed wire in the gaps between buildings. Things seemed ordinary enough on the surface, but the tension was thick.

"Welcome to Fort Zinderneuf," K'nidMin said to her. "That's what the humans named this place." She hardly needed her empathic talent to sense his disapproval. "Most of this was their bright idea." He gestured broadly at the defenses. "Still, until we can connect with the Flyers, it's a sensible precaution."

There was more to it than that. Their collective aura of fear put her nerves on edge. "Sensible? These people are scared. What do you define as 'sensible'?"

K'nidMin glanced at her. "You feel it, hmm? Once you've seen the Flyers you'll understand."

§

There was a welcoming committee waiting for them, and K'nidMin made introductions all around. "This is my Worthy." He pointed out a bulky fellow with a cool expression. "Learnéd C'venBren is our xenosociologist and you already know Learnéd Z'gehRoo. Specialist B'genMos handles communications and Specialist A'vemDrem is our intelligence analyst."

They were an odd lot, to say the least. C'venBren was elderly and seemed infirm, much like Z'gehRoo, while the two Specialists were typical of the 'Dark Grays' rankers she'd met in the past. Both eyed her with interest, and their auras made her uncomfortable.

"So this is your special talent?" the Worthy said.

"What? You've heard about her?"

"A supply ship came in a few days back. She was mentioned in the latest communique, although they didn't provide any details." He pondered her with a skeptical ear twitch. "This wasn't what you went to d'enchia for."

"She was a lucky find. She received a telepathic upgrade from J J Ballas, and thus far seems to be handling it well."

"Thus far," Learnéd Z'geghRoo said, skeptically. "I sincerely hope so, but I want to run a standard spectrum on her to make sure she's alright before turning her loose in the field."

"I am not *er'trxxda*, if that's what you think!" she snapped at him.

"I meant no disrespect," he offered, hastily. "But the powers you possess have a profound impact on the mind. We need to monitor you closely to guard against any bad effects."

She knew the truth of *that* all too well. Having him on hand reassured her, although the idea of having her own personal psychiatrist in attendance was a bit disconcerting.

"Well I hope she can do some good," the Worthy grumbled. "Things are falling apart here, and unless we make some progress soon, we might as well give up."

"We're not licked yet," K'nidMin said, firmly.

"Not yet," his Worthy muttered.

§

Their next stop was the office grotto shared by the Ic'nichi Arbiter and the human Ambassador. Arbiter G'nemBrik squatted at a metal folding table poking at a plate of *uf'thoka* and mystery meat which he clearly wasn't enjoying. "Did you bring any *'sti'eit* this trip?" he demanded when they came in.

K'nidMin offered an amused ear twitch. "You can relax, sir. There's a pallet of it on the ship."

G'nemBrik sighed. "You might have brought a few cartons down. I could use a good, cold *'sti'eit* about now." He shoved his plate aside and pondered R'nemReth with little enthusiasm. "So this is your special talent? She seems awfully young for something like this."

"There is no formal age policy for possessing psychic powers, sir," K'nidMin said, firmly. "She showed some major abilities on Checkpoint, and we're still exploring what she can do. We can count on her to get through to the Flyers."

"So I was told in the latest dispatches. I hope she can do some good, because I hear you got *n'vebRnng* otherwise." He sighed in obvious despair. "The humans dropped our pallet of *'sti'eit,* too. What a waste."

"I was given precious little joy this last trip, but we seem to be drawing attention in the World Nest. Hopefully R'nemReth's discovery is a positive sign."

"Maybe not. The dispatch made it clear they expect results or they will shut us down." He pondered R'nemReth skeptically. "Can she deliver?"

"She received a telepathic upgrade from J J Ballas; he knows far more about this than we ever will."

"That one." G'nemBrik sighed, and his ears reclined in dismay. "Their powers make me nervous." He paused to size R'nemReth up with a skeptical eye. "I hope they know what they're doing."

They were interrupted when a large, heavyset human came in. "Ahh! Mister K'nidMin. You're back I see."

"You see correctly." K'nidMin's tone and aura were both cool. "R'nemReth, this is Sir Miles Willoughby, the human Arbiter."

"Ambassador, sir, Ambassador! Do please get the title correct."

They were an odd pair, to say the least. Arbiter G'nemBrik was elderly and stringy, with a thin snout, prominent ears and a beaten look; your typical bureaucrat. *Ambassador* Sir Miles Willoughby was ponderous and florid, with a voice which carried and a personality to match. He collapsed onto a folding chair which threatened to collapse under him in turn. "I hope you bring good news," he grumbled. "Morale here is in the basement between this weather and your lack of progress."

"Well you can relax, sir. We received an unexpected addition to our herd; R'nemReth. She was gifted with telepathy by J J Ballas, so she can communicate with the Flyers directly."

Sir Miles pondered her skeptically, his aura bordering on hostile. "Did he? Why doesn't that...person...that J J do this? He's a lot better at this than any of you will ever be."

"Unfortunately, from what I was told, the Dreamsingers aren't able to remain in contact with non-telepaths for any length of time," G'nemBrik said. "Pity: this would be a whole lot simpler if we could get them to do the heavy lifting."

Sir Miles' aura turned cool. "To be honest, I would rather not depend on *them* to run our foreign policy, a position Geneva strongly shares."

"Fortunately we won't have to," G'nemBrik said with labored patience. "We have our own telepath now, so hopefully the contact herd can finally make a breakthrough."

"It's all a lot of ignorant hocus-pocus!" Sir Miles grumbled.

'R'nemReth, talk to them,' K'nidMin's thought came to her.

"I don't see why we can trust these Dreamsingers any more than the Flyers," Sir Miles went on. "It's all alien nonsense..."

'You are wrong.' Her thought brought the debate to a stunned halt. *'These Dreamsingers...they're really powerful. They scare me, they're so powerful. They say I can do this, and we have every reason to think it'll work.'*

There was a long moment of stunned silence. "Can you be sure of your power?" Arbiter G'nemBrik asked. "I imagine this telepathy can overwhelm you at times. Can you control it when you make contact with them?"

She wasn't happy to be the center of attention at a moment like this, but she put aside her doubts. There was work to do. *'Yes, I have a hard time controlling it,'* she thought. *'It's so potent it takes my full concentration. But I've worked hard on the exercises. I can handle it. If anyone can talk with the Flyers, it's me.'*

"Plus she'll be away from the camp, so there won't be so many random minds to interfere," K'nidMin added. "We came here for a purpose. If we are to succeed, we need to take her out there." He drilled the leadership with a stern glare. "I have faith in her, as should you. It won't be *our* fault if we fail!"

§

"So *they're* the brains of this stampede?" R'nemReth grumbled after they left the office grotto.

"I wouldn't say 'brains' is the right term," K'nidMin said. "They're both political appointees. Our First Contact herd doesn't enjoy universal favor, so many of those assigned to us are, shall we say, less than stellar."

"Do you think they will shut us down?" That dispatch from home was ominous; she wondered if the Ki-Elder had a hand in it.

K'nidMin offered a vexed ear twitch. "I wouldn't be surprised. We've been here forever with nothing to show for it." He paused and pondered the question. "Still...they went to a lot of effort to send you here, so they probably won't do anything as long as we're making progress."

"Or as long as we're not forced to admit defeat."

"Same thing."

A moment later they ran into two humans. "This is Lieutenant Ellesse Horton," K'nidMin introduced the smaller one. "She's the leader of their half of the Contact Herd."

She? So this was a human female, the first R'nemReth met. She was short for a human, lean and wiry, with close-cropped pale yellow fur, and R'nemReth could feel the toughness in her aura. This was not a fem to mess with. "So you're our new team member?" she said. "Welcome to hell!"

"She doesn't speak human," K'nidMin said. "But she can communicate telepathically."   He turned his attention to R'nemReth. *'Try using your repeating ability'*, he thought to her. *'Let's see if it can work across languages.'*

R'nemReth repeated his thought. *'Hmph! That's a neat trick!'* Horton replied.   It seemed they could understand each other perfectly even through the language barrier. *'That'll prove a useful talent in this Fuster Cluck.'* She smiled at R'nemReth. *'We might actually do some good around here, now that you're with us.'*

Her praise and welcoming aura felt good, and R'nemReth took a liking to her right off; the first human she'd met yet who she felt comfortable with.

'And this is her second, Sargent MacIntosh.'   K'nidMin gestured to the large, stocky human.

'Um...hello.' R'nemReth was bemused by the sight. He was wearing a standard human fatigue jacket above, but his legs were encased in a simple cloth tube decorated with an ornate broach rather than trousers. *'Don't you get cold in that...thing?'*

MacIntosh gave her a superior look. *'Tis a kilt, lassie. And a r-r-real mon dinna fash himself or' the weather.'*

Horton was amused. *'That's the Scots for you.   Mad as a Hatter, all of them. It's what makes them such formidable fighters.'*

'Aye. That and a wee drop of single malt.'

R'nemReth had no idea what a Hatter or single malt were, and from the steely look in his eye she wasn't anxious to find out. *'Um...well, I'm pleased to meet you.'*

'So how have things been while we were gone?' K'nidMin asked.

Horton snorted in contempt. *'The usual: panic, wetness, and running in circles. Too much rain, too much headwind from the higher-ups, precious little progress to brag on.'*

'So Sir Miles Wannabee is at it again, hmmm?'

'He's achieved glorious new heights of dithering!'

K'nidMin laughed. *'I see I missed all the excitement.'*

"Lieutenant Horton!" They were interrupted by a large human in military fatigues who hesitated when he saw K'nidMin. "You're back, huh? Did you have any luck?"

"Some," K'nidMin greeted him coolly. "This is R'nemReth. She's been assigned to our herd. R'nemReth, this is Captain Pencroft, commanding the human forces and Lieutenant Horton's immediate superior."

Pencroft eyed her skeptically. "So what does she do?"

"She's a telepath. J J Ballas outfitted her so she can link with the Flyers."

His aura was a mix of disbelief and contempt. "A telepath, huh? Gawd, that's about what I've come to expect from this Fuster Cluck!"

"But she's..."

"And you're dorking around with those Dreamsingers again. That's no more than we can expect from you lizards!" He gave her a sour look and went on his way.

'Where does he come off with that 'lizard' remark?' R'nemReth demanded after he left. *'That was un'brapta!'*

'Sorry,' Horton said, quietly. *'The only thing 'superior' about him is his rank.'*

'He can be s'vem'grott at times,' K'nidMin added. *'Don't let him get under your scales.'*

They were interrupted again by a ringing alarm. "First stage alert," MacIntosh said. "There are Flyers out there."

K'nidMin turned to R'nemReth. "Come on. You'll want to see this."

They trotted toward the perimeter, and climbed up to an observation post on the roof of a warehouse. Half way between the camp and the distant herd, a hand's worth of Flyers drifted back and forth, their broad wings catching the thermals. Even way off in the distance, they were a sight to behold: pale gray on their undersides, darker gray-brown above, drifting effortlessly on the chill air as they wheeled back and forth along a line drawn across the prairie.

"What are they doing?" R'nemReth asked.

Specialist A'vemDrem stood nearby snapping photos with an enormous telephoto lens. "They're a picket line," he said. "It's something they started doing recently; patrolling to keep us away from the hunt."

Further away, the herd was milling around in panic as another hand's worth of Flyers hovered over them. As they watched, one swooped down and came away with one of the beasts, flapping his wings hard to climb with the heavy load. The sight dismayed R'nemReth: they could easily carry someone her size away.

Another Flyer made his catch and departed. The other two followed, then the picket line broke off one by one and took their catches until the last of them was receding toward the mountains in the distance.

'That's intelligent behavior if ever there was such,' Lieutenant Horton said.

'Organized and disciplined,' K'nidMin added. *'They operate as a hunting pack.'* He turned to R'nemReth. *'Those are your quarry.'*

'Wonderful.' She was dismayed at the size and power of the creatures, and by how purposeful they were in their bloody effort. She could see why everyone here was afraid of them.

§

After the last flyer left, K'nidMin led her to a barracks and a private room. It was little more than a cubical, bare and functional with a necessary minimum of furnishings, but at least she was quartered under a solid roof, which she was thankful for.

"I need to match ears with our herd," he told her. "You have a little time to settle in before late-meal is ready."

Once he was gone, she sagged on the bed in dismay. "*l'cc'vn* she mumbled. "What have I got myself into?"

There were no answers to be found by staring at the wall, and the silence left her feeling lost. After a bit she noticed the sound of rain drumming on the roof. That reminded her of late-meal, which reminded her she existed on endurance rations for twelve *Ancestorless* days. She crawled to her feet and made her way to the base cafeteria, hoping her luck would improve over what she'd seen thus far.

The cafeteria was basic: another prefab metal building, a jury-rigged serving line, and the selection wasn't promising, but it beat endurance rations. She filled her plate, helped herself to a bowl of *V'liz*, and settled at one of the trestle tables with both Ic'nichi and human seating.

A bit later Lieutenant Horton came by. *'So how are you doing?'* she thought as she settled nearby.

'I am managing, thank you.' Right then she was grateful for a bit of company. *'I miss my home world.'*

'I know how you feel. Space is vast and lonely, and this is hardly prime real estate.' She helped herself to a bite of her meal. *'I understand you are still young. This must be quite an adventure for you.'*

'If it is, I'm not enjoying it.'

'Not surprising. An adventure is when you're having a bad time in a nasty place far from home.' She offered a smile, and her aura was warm and supportive. *'We'll look out for you.'*

'Thank you.' Her encouragement felt good, and it was nice to have someone who cared about her.

'So how do you like your boss?' She smiled at R'nemReth's confused look. *'K'nidMin.'*

'That one! He thinks highly of himself.'

'He does. Still, he's a likable sort. A girl could do worse.'

'You can be his mate, then!'

Horton's aura lit up. *'So, he is interested, isn't he?'*

'I didn't say that.'

'Relax, kiddo. He's kind of obvious around you, is all.'

R'nemReth withdrew a bit. *'All I want is to get this done so I can go home. I don't want to get involved with him, or anybody else.'*

'You miss your friends, don't you?'

That struck a bitter note with her. *'I don't have any friends back on d'enchia.'*

'No one?' Horton's aura was sympathetic. *'That's sad. At least you have friends here with us.'* R'nemReth could tell Horton was including herself in that. *'And it wouldn't hurt to give K'nidMin a chance. He's a decent sort.'*

'Well...he is interested in me...I can hear his thoughts.'

She grinned. *'One of the fringe benefits of telepathy, I suppose. Not that we girls need it when it comes to men.'*

K'nidMin came by just then with his tray. "So how are you two getting on?" he asked Horton.

Horton withdrew a bit and offered a coy smile. "Oh, we're just indulging in a bit of girl-talk."

"I can well imagine." He settled opposite them. *'How are you doing, R'nemReth?'* he thought.

'I'm fine, thank you.'

'So how do you propose we put her to work?' Horton asked.

'We need to approach to within her range so she can contact the Flyers.'

'How close is that?'

K'nidMin hesitated. *'We still don't know. It's something we need to look into. In any case, once we get their attention, we can set up a meeting and bring in the tail-shakers.'*

Horton made a snort of contempt. *'That lot!'*

'They're what we have. If they botch it, it won't be our fault.'

Horton mused over the prospect. *'I doubt if the Flyers will be very receptive during one of their hunts. We may need to go out and try to locate some random individual.'*

R'nemReth was not thrilled to have them planning out her future, especially as it was starting to sound risky. *'Will that be dangerous?'*

Horton laid a comforting hand on hers. *'We'll protect you. Our teams have the firepower to extract ourselves if need be.'*

'Let's hope it doesn't come to that,' K'nidmin thought. *'But we should set up a few joint drills to get everyone galloping together.'*

'Agreed. It'll get Pencroft off our backs at least.'

They were interrupted just then by Captain Pencroft. "I trust you two have your teams in gear?" he demanded.

"We are ready for any productive effort," K'nidMin said, firmly. Horton nodded in agreement.

"A waste of time," he grumbled. "Those animals are dangerous. We ought to write them off and get to work colonizing, not that this world is worth the effort anyway."

"They are reasoning beings," K'nidMin protested. "It wouldn't be right to exterminate them and take their world."

"Reasoning beings, eh?" Pencroft gave him a sour look. "Just be thankful they don't have star travel! In any case, this is our stellar zone, so you lizards don't need to worry about soiling your pretty little hands!"

"Sorry," Horton muttered after he left.

'Please be patient with him,' K'nidMin thought to R'nemReth. *'The humans have a long tradition that any creature harming one of them must be destroyed. Their law is different with intelligent beings, of course, but there have been tragedies in their past.'*

'He's not a shining example of our kind,' Horton grumbled.

'What is his problem?'

'A human from the original landing party was killed by the Flyers,' K'nidMin thought. *'He seems perpetually upset by it.'*

'It must have been a mistake,' Horton objected. *'They never saw humans before; how would they know?'*

'We wouldn't know about them either if J J Ballas hadn't stepped in.'

'Precisely. That's why it's so important to get this program working. Our two races almost went to war when the First Contact was botched. We can't afford any more mistakes.'

'Especially if we do run into a star-traveling race.' K'nidMin's aura turned chilly at the thought, as did Horton's.

'Someone once said that if we go out into the Universe acting like savages, someday we'll meet someone capable of treating us as savages.' Horton's aura turned even more gloomy. *'There's way too much of that in our past. We need to better ourselves if we're to survive in the long run.'*

K'nidMin sighed. *'Still, you humans are very emotional, and many of you don't handle upsetting events well. His reaction is understandable.'* He turned to R'nemReth. *'You might keep that in mind around him, at least for now.'*

'There is the sad truth.' Horton's aura was tinged with regret. *'I only hope he'll get over it, in time.'*

*****

"First Attempts"

"You'll get yourselves killed," Captain Pencroft said, sharply, as the contact herd hastily gathered at the gate the next morning while another Flyer hunt was getting under way. "We don't dare go out beyond the fence except in force with all *them* out there."

"We have an edge now." K'nidMin gestured to R'nemReth, hovering in the background. "She can reach out to them telepathically."

"If the Dreamsingers say she can communicate with them, then we must assume she can, sir," Horton added.

Pencroft showed his opinion of the Dreamsingers with a snort of contempt. "You are fools to believe them. You're likely to die for it."

"We have more faith in ourselves, sir," K'nidMin said. His unspoken *'...than you do'* hung in the air between them.

"Enough bickering!" Arbiter G'nemBrik said. "It has to be tried, so let's get to it and hope for the best."

"We better move," Horton said. In the distance the hunt was shaping up rapidly. The Flyer picket line was already established, and the herd beasts were being chased into a compact, milling mass as the Flyers prepared to strike.

"Good luck to you all," G'nemBrik said. "I hope you are successful."

"Thank you, Arbiter." K'nidMin gathered up his courage and headed out, followed by Horton and the rest.

§

The weather was overcast, with occasional chilly sprinkles and patches of ground fog. Even at mid-morning the daylight was subdued under solid cloud cover. The undergrowth was dripping wet over thick boggy mud so that once beyond the gate their progress was slow and unpleasant.

"Does it ever stop raining here?" R'nemReth complained. Her footsocks were soaked, chilling her, and the clinging mud was revolting.

"I think it did once," K'nidMin grumbled. "But I couldn't swear to it."

"Don't bet your paycheck on it," Horton muttered. If anything the humans were having a harder time since the Ic'nichi had the broad splayed feet of their primitive bog-dwelling ancestors. The humans also suffered from the chill while the Ic'nichi were overheating. Horton and her herd were miserable, and a couple of them were trembling from the cold.

"I hate this place!" R'nemReth griped. "Why couldn't you bring the Flyers to Checkpoint so we could deal with them in comfort?"

"That's a good idea," K'nidMin said, shortly. "Why don't you submit it through channels?"

She bit back a sharp retort, carefully dodged a stickly bush, and trudged on, fuming.

They made poor time due to the mud. As much as K'nidMin and Horton wanted to race ahead, they were forced to slow down so the civilian herd members, most of whom were elderly, could keep up. Fortunately the hunt shaping up ahead was huge; it might have been over by time they arrived otherwise.

"What do you make of all that?" Horton gestured to the swarming Flyers. The picket line was far more extensive than before, and there were still plenty of them to corral the herd beasts. "I estimate a couple dozen of them at least."

"That's probably their entire tribe," Learnéd C'venBren said, uneasily. "They must be up to something special; taking that much meat all at once would be counterproductive unless they thought there'd be a shortage soon."

"Could they be stocking up for winter?" Doctor Lassiter, the human team's xenosociologist, asked. "Those carcasses would keep if left in the snow at higher altitudes."

"Perhaps they anticipate storms which will make flying hazardous," C'venBren replied. "We should check the long range forecasts to see if blizzards are coming in."

The picket line of Flyers reacted as they drew closer, shifting their path to block the way forward. As they marched on, the Flyers began bending their flight path into a semicircle, and a steady trickle of reinforcements joined them so that when the contact herd finally called a halt, they were flanked on three sides.

"I suspect it isn't wise to go any further," Horton said, uneasily. The picket line was only a few hundred lengths above them and not much further away, and the additions from the hunting party were extending either flank.

K'nidMin was uneasy as well. "This will have to do." He turned to R'nemReth. "Can you reach them from here?"

She was frankly terrified by the creatures circling overhead. The Flyers were impressive from a distance; up close, the sight was intimidating. "I...should be able to."

'You can do this,' K'nidMin's thought came to her.

'I guess I better, before they do something.' She tried to clear her mind of confusion and fear, and reached out to the nearest Flyer. *'Can you hear me? We want to talk to you.'*

No reaction. The picket line continued to circle above them, stretching now to three sides in depth.

'Please talk to us. We want to be your friends.'

No response, even though she repeated her thought several times with various Flyers. They ignored her, and kept circling.

'Can we please speak with your leaders? We have important things to discuss.'

One of the Flyers emitted a sharp cry, and the flanks began edging closer. "They're almost surrounding us," Horton said. They were all but cut off from their line of retreat.

A'vemDrem was busy with his huge telephoto lens again. "No! Don't use that thing now!" Horton said. "They might mistake it for a weapon." A'vemDrem flinched, then hastily stowed his camera in its carrying case.

'We mean you no harm! Please listen!'

"Ah dinna like this. We best nae press our luck," Sergeant MacIntosh said. Even as he did, one of the Flyers crossed the gap to the other flank, showing how close they were to being encircled.

"That's a final warning." K'nidMin' Worthy was worried. "Can you get through to them?" he asked R'nemReth.

'Please talk to us,' she pleaded with the ominous shapes all but overhead. *'We want to be your friends.'*

They offered no response except to edge lower as they circled. "I can't reach them," she said. "They aren't listening."

72

With that, the Flyers completed their circle, drifting completely around them. "We have to break off and withdraw," Horton said. Her aura, and the aura of the contact herd in general was thick with fear. They were trapped unless the Flyers decided to let them go. The armed members of both races were nervously fingering their weapons. At this range against these numbers, their limited firepower was not enough to save them.

"Right," K'nidMin said at last. "Everyone move back in formation, nice and slow. No weapons."

That took some doing since the humans were on the edge of panic, not that the Ic'nichi were much calmer. The herd moved back one reluctant step at a time, a circular formation guarding all sides as they tried to hold together. The Flyers followed, circling completely around them now, adjusting their courses to stay with the contact herd as they retreated.

"We're going to lose it," Horton muttered, tensely. Their formation was becoming ragged as the pace faltered.

"Stand fast, lads!" Sargent MacIntosh called out. "Dinna show them yer heels." One of the humans was starting to panic. "Keep t' ranks there, Private Mahmud! Ye dinna want t' disgrace the r-r-regiment!"

'R'nemReth, repeat this,' K'nidMin ordered. *'All of you stay in formation. If we break and scatter, it'll set them off.'*

Somehow they held together although on the edge of panic as they retreated several hundred lengths, with Sargent MacIntosh and K'nidMin's Worthy barking orders and encouragement all the while. The Flyers eventually broke off their circular formation and reestablished their picket line, and the Contact Herd beat a hasty retreat.

§

"We saw the whole thing," Sir Miles said when they met in the office grotto after returning. "You were lucky to get out of that alive!"

K'nidMin and Lieutenant Horton were standing before the ad-hoc leadership committee of the two diplomats and the two military leaders, who were not pleased with their failure. "They were warning us off," K'nidMin said with more conviction than he felt at the moment. "They could have attacked, but didn't. Once we backed down, they let us go."

"They were intimidated by your weapons," Captain Pencroft said, sharply. "They would have gotten up the nerve to attack you sooner or later, and nothing could have saved you!"

"I disagree, sir," K'nidMin said, firmly. "I was there; you weren't. My assessment was they were trying to force us away."

"I concur, sir," Horton added.

"This bickering is pointless," Arbiter G'nemBrik said. "What matters is they rejected your overture, so what do we do now?"

"It's obvious," Sir Miles said. "Your telepath failed. Our last prospect was unsuccessful. All that remains now is to admit failure and evacuate."

"I'm afraid Sir Miles is right," G'nemBrik added. "Your teams gave it an heroic effort, but it just didn't work."

§

"I don't know what to do now," K'nidMin sighed.

He, Horton, Sergeant MacIntosh, K'nidMin's Worthy and R'nemReth were sheltering from the steady drizzle under the awning in front of the Admin grotto to try to figure out their next move. It didn't look promising.

"It's hopeless," Horton said. "I'm fresh out of ideas."

"Aye, sometimes the cards just dinna come t' yer hand," Sergeant MacIntosh added. "We canna win every battle."

"Sad but true," K'nidMin's Worthy grumbled. "The Ancestors aren't smiling at us, so we simply have to accept it."

"It's just...I hate the thought of failing." K'nidMin's aura was morose, and R'nemReth could tell he was concerned about her.

The thought of failure, especially when so much depended on her, left her depressed and lonely, so much that she was overcome by the need to reach out to the only person who could help her...as frightening as he was. *'J J,'* she thought. *'Did I do something wrong? This telepathy isn't working.'*

A warm sense of peace and confidence flooded into her, calming her fear and damping down her despair. *'You did fine, Lil-Missy. Yo' telepathy is working fine too. Don't you fret none. They just wasn't listenin' is all.'*

74

A'vemDrem came trotting up. "I checked the forecast, sir. They say they don't have enough data to make long range predictions, but the weather does seem to be entering a winter phase. Whether that means snow or more rain is unknown, sir."

K'nidMin nodded, his aura morose and frustrated. A'vemDrem's report confirmed his worse suspicions about the Flyers' massive hunt. With the weather worsening, their chances of success were dwindling down to nothing.

"So now what?" Horton asked.

K'nidMin stared at the dirty gray sky for some time, his angst and frustration plain to see. "I have no idea," he said at last. "We failed. I guess it's over."

That stirred R'nemReth to act. *'No, it's not,'* she thought. *'J J said they weren't listening.'*

K'nidMin'a aura erupted with confusion and excitement. "What? You're sure about that?"

'Yes. He said my telepathy is working fine.'

"Then why didn't they respond?" Horton asked.

'I don't know.' Her thought was tinged with frustration.

"We're missing something." K'nidMin stood stock still, thinking fast, the turmoil in his mind spilling out of him. "There has to be something...we just have to find it..." He cursed the Flyers for their stubbornness, cursed the so-called leadership for giving up so easily. "Call everyone together," he said at last. "We need to talk this out."

§

"There has to be *something*," K'nidMin muttered. "Some detail we missed. But what?" The joint contact herd was gathered in the cafeteria for a council of war, trying to come up with an answer to the riddle of the Flyers' rejection to their appeal. K'nidMin was pacing back and forth in frustration, his aura dripping with angst, his thoughts in turmoil.

"Maybe they simply don't want to talk with us," Horton said. "We can't get through to them."

"We don't know that," Learnéd C'venBren said. "There may be some sort of spiritual significance to their hunt, and they resented our interfering."

75

"I concur with my colleague," Doctor Lassiter said. "Food gathering is always a critical matter for primitive people. The size of the hunting party suggests they may have been gathering food for the winter."

K'nidMin grabbed that. "We know it wasn't R'nemReth's failure, so they must have a reason for not responding."

"It may have been their hunt, or it could be their mating season, or they may have some ideological reason not to communicate with us. Perhaps they disrespect us since we can't fly. There's no way of knowing."

Horton gave R'nemReth a sympathetic glance. "Granted. But what do we do? We *have* to connect with them."

"There's only one thing we can do," K'nidMin said. "We need to take an expedition into Flyer country."

"Into the mountains?"

"Up into the hills anyway, as far as we must to get their attention. Then they can't ignore us."

"That's risky, sir," A'vemDrem said. "They may not react as we hope. If we go in force, they'll either attack or avoid us, and our herd by itself is too small for an adequate defense."

"It's risky, true, but it's our only option." K'nidMin confronted the others. "I know this is a gamble, but I can't see any alternative. Will you go with me?"

There was an uncomfortable silence as they pondered the odds. But such was the strength of his appeal that, one by one, they agreed to follow him and Horton on what could be a suicide mission.

"You still have to sell this idea to the front office," Horton said. "That's going to take some doing."

"Maybe I can help with them," R'nemReth said.

§

"You want to go out there *again*?" Arbiter G'nemBrik was dismayed by the joint herd's request when they reconvened later that afternoon. "You've already failed. What good can you do?"

"We believe the failure may have been due to circumstances, sir," K'nidMin said. "We want to try another approach." He and Horton were confronting the base leadership again while

R'nemReth listened in from the outer room, ready to act as their strategic edge.

"We have nearly a month until the next transport arrives, and it will take longer to arrange to have the missions withdrawn," Horton said. "Until then, we need to keep trying."

"Absolutely not!" Sir Miles huffed. "It's a waste of time and a potential waste of lives. I won't agree to it!"

'He's going to be trouble,' R'nemReth thought to K'nidMin and Horton. *'Focus on his lack of courage.'*

"We have plenty of time, Ambassador," K'nidMin said, firmly. "And our lives are our own. We're willing to take the gamble."

"Nonsense! You are a soldier, sir," Captain Pencroft snapped. "All of you have duties to your people, and can't go tossing your lives away no matter how devoted you are!"

"Plus you have several civilians in your charge, including your supposed telepath," Sir Miles added. "Your *duty* is to protect them by staying put!"

'You almost had Sir Miles, if Pencroft hadn't started chasing his own tail!'

'He's not our only problem child,' Horton thought.

First Degree E'zemBron didn't say anything, but was following the discussion closely with a skeptical aura which was shifting by degrees. *'E'zemBron is wavering,'* R'nemReth thought to K'nidMin and Horton. *'Focus on his sense of duty.'*

K'nidMin followed up smartly. "Our teams are all volunteers and professionals, sir," he said to Pencroft, evenly. "In our *professional* opinion there is still a chance to make contact. It is our *duty*, the *duty* of this First Contact herd, to try."

'That did it. You have E'zemBron, but handle him carefully.'

"I must agree with K'nidMin," E'zemBron said, reluctantly. "They are the experts. They're here to do an important job, and if they're willing to risk it, we should let them."

"You can't be serious!" Sir Miles objected.

E'zemBron gave him a hard glare as his aura shifted toward anger. "I can if I want to!"

K'nidMin offered a fervent mental prayer of thanks for Sir Miles' belligerence. "*Think* of it, sir! The Flyers aren't the issue here. This is a test case to develop an effective First Contact program. As long as there are *any* options, we *must* explore them!"

'That scored with E'zemBron!'

"We'll meet other star-traveling races someday," E'zemBron said, sternly. "We already had one botched contact which nearly led to interstellar war. We can't afford another. If they think they can get results, we have to let them try."

'The Arbiter is wavering too. Sir Miles is uncertain.'

"Even if we fail again, we gain useful experience," Horton added. "It's better to develop our technique here with these primitives, even if it means risking lives, than trying to ad-hoc something when we meet more star-travelers."

'That worries Sir Miles.' They were all thankful for E'zemBron's defection, which was weakening the others.

"First Degree E'zemBron was right about the risk of interstellar war," K'nidMin said to Pencroft. "Our two races are still troubled by that fiasco. Not only do we need better contact methods, but this project is also intended to help heal the rift."

"Well..." G'nemBrik muttered. "You do make some good points."

'You have him, and Sir Miles is wavering.'

They were getting close. K'nidMin played a strategic card. "In any case, it'll look bad in your reports, to both governments, if we spend all this time standing on our tails waiting to be evacuated without trying again."

'That did it!'

The leadership circle hemmed and hawed for some time before coming to the only possible decision. "It seems you make a persuasive argument," Arbiter G'nemBrik said at last. "You might as well continue your efforts until the evacuation can be arranged."

Sir Miles was not pleased at being outmaneuvered. "So what are your plans, now that you have the go-ahead?" he demanded.

'Don't discuss that with them!'

K'nidMin backtracked smoothly. "Ah...we aren't entirely sure yet." He exchanged glances with Horton. "We're still considering various options."

§

The two linked up with R'nemReth after the meeting broke up. "We did it!" Horton cheered. "Your insight made it happen."

K'nidMin greeted her with an aura of warm approval. "Forget what I said about losing you to the diplomats. You're much too useful at getting them out of the way!"

R'nemReth didn't entirely share their enthusiasm. "Yes, well, now we have to make good on your promises. Let's just hope Sir Miles is proven wrong."

"You would do better to put your hopes in the Flyers than in Sir Miles," Horton said. "There is more in this Universe than you can imagine."

They were interrupted by the most horrendous sound R'nemReth could imagine. "What is *that?!*" she asked in alarm.

K'nidMin pointed to where Sergeant MacIntosh was standing on the observation deck, outlined by the fading twilight, with an ornately decorated bag with several pipes coming out of it tucked under one arm. He was blowing into one pipe while fingering it, producing an Ancestorless wailing noise.

"*What* is he doing?"

"Amazing Grace, I think," K'nidMin said. "It's hard to tell one song from another."

She turned to him, incredulous. "*That's* music?"

"The humans seem to think so, most of them." He gestured at two humans standing nearby listening raptly. "I sometimes wonder if these Scots are a whole separate species who only look human."

"They might be," she mumbled. *'You humans are er'trxxda, every last one of you!'* she thought to Horton.

Horton replied with an amused snort. *'Yes, we are. Isn't it exciting?'*

'That depends on what you consider 'excitement'.

Still...as she listened to the eerie sound, the damp chill sent a shiver through her. She sensed a fleeting, emotionally charged image of the Sergeant's 'Scotland' in Hortons thoughts: it disturbed her and fascinated her at the same time. Horton was right: there was more to this Universe than she ever imagined.

*****

"A Desperate Ploy"

"If we're going to contact them, we need to go to them," K'nidMin said, reasonably. He and Lieutenant Horton were standing before the ad-hoc leadership circle for the third time that day. It was time to reveal their plans—and hope for the best. "They won't come near the encampment, and they won't let us near their hunting expeditions, so we need to reach out to them."

"This is folly!" Sir Miles objected. "You'd be way beyond any hope of aid if you run into trouble, and I, for one, wouldn't agree to attempting a rescue mission!"

His obvious willingness to write them off rankled, but the Contact Herd leaders didn't let it deter them. "*We* are *prepared* to take the chance, even if *you* are not!" Horton said, sternly. Sir Miles wilted under her glare.

"Perhaps if they were better armed?" First Degree E'zemBron was not thrilled by their proposal, but his tail was stiff enough that he would at least discuss it. "If they draw from the heavy weapons stock, they'll be able to inflict severe losses on any attack. It would force the Flyers to break off and let them escape."

"Sir, all that firepower would be counterproductive," K'nidMin objected.

"Nonetheless, it may be your lifeline."

Of the four leaders, Arbiter G'nemBrik was wavering, Captain Pencroft dismissed it outright, E'zemBron was doubtful...and Sir Miles persisted in objecting long and loud. By mutual agreement, breaking his resistance was the key. "We are confident we can do this, sir," K'nidMin said to E'zemBron as he kept his empathy trained on Sir Miles. "They haven't attacked us yet, and we feel they won't unless we directly threaten them."

"Plus it is our duty to take risks, calculated risks, to gain a needed result," Horton added. "We can make this work."

"And we have R'nemReth," K'nidMin said. "Her telepathy gives us the edge we need."

"Still, I can't agree to it," Sir Miles said. "The Flyers have shown us that we are unwelcome, and it is foolish to risk their wrath by invading their territory!"

K'nidMin fixed him with a stern glare. "Sir, are you prepared to report to your government that the Contact Herd gave up after a simple threat display *on your orders?*"

§

"I hope you know what you're doing," Arbiter G'nemBrik said as the joint Contact Herd gathered at the perimeter gate the next morning. The leadership reluctantly approved their plan, with a host of conditions and after long argument, and they were anxious to 'get the hell out'a Dodge' as Horton put it before their support crumbled.

"Relax, sir," K'nidMin said. "We've got the right knot for this tail." He gestured at R'nemReth. "Have the victory parade ready when we return."

G'nemBrik's ears fluttered in turn. "I admire your *l'fru'ng* anyway. I just hope Ambassador Willoughby is proven wrong." In fact, Sir Miles gave his consent to the mission solely due to the implied threat of scandal, which was the only reason Captain Pencroft was overruled.

K'nidMin offered a snort of self-assured contempt he didn't really feel. "Don't worry, sir. We'll be back tomorrow at the latest."

"Are you really going to leave all that weaponry behind?" G'nemBrik asked, plaintively. "You may need it, you know. Better safe than sorry." The Contact Herd made a fine show of armed bravado until the other leaders left, then secreted their heavy weapons and the bulky radio in a convenient storeroom.

"They'll slow us down, sir, plus we really don't want to present such an image to the Flyers. Our regular issue will be sufficient."

"I sincerely hope so," G'nemBrik sighed. "Sir Miles will be impossible if you get killed."

"We have more confidence in ourselves than Sir Miles does," K'nidMin said, firmly. "We know what we're doing." With that he turned and led the joint Contact Herd out the gate and into the tangled prairie undergrowth.

"We do know what we're doing, don't we?" Horton asked after they left the compound.

"I sincerely hope so," K'nidMin muttered.

"At least we don't have to lug all those munitions around." The human concept of 'heavy weapons' would have doubled their load.

"Oy," K'nidMin grumbled the popular human term.

She glanced at him. "Oy, indeed."

§

They set a steady pace, K'nidMin and Horton in the lead, R'nemReth right behind, and the remainder strung out in two columns. Thirteen people altogether to confront an alien race on their home turf. The weather was brisk with an onshore breeze sending high clouds drifting ahead of them.

"Do you think it'll rain?" Horton asked.

"I checked the weather," K'nidMin said. "There's another storm brewing out to sea, but no word on when or if it'll get here. We should have several days yet if it does."

"Good. I don't need another head cold." She rubbed her hands together and studied the sky. "It's like autumn back home, but without the trees turning colors. I miss that."

Curious, R'nemReth peered into her mind and caught fleeting glimpses of a vast forest with leaves a riot of color. *'So that's what red is like,'* she thought. It was alien; beautiful, but alien.

"What's the hurry?" Learnéd Z'gehRoo grumbled from the mid-ranks. "We'll never catch them if they choose to fly away."

That was met with a chorus of muttering from the rest of them. "You're right," K'nidMin said. "We've gone far enough that we don't need to worry about them calling us back." His convenient explanation didn't mask his aura of embarrassment. "We'll take it easier from here."

They continued at a slower pace for the civilians. "My mistake," he muttered to Horton. "I'm not used to long marches with a mixed force."

"Don't let it bother you," Horton mumbled back. "Civilians in the ranks are always a headache. Besides, long marches are tough on everyone."

Right behind them, R'nemReth overheard their conversation, but chose not to make anything of it. If long marches were called for, there was no sense getting *r'vebbe* over it.

§

By mid-afternoon they were well on their way inland. They came to the end of the flat coastal plain, and entered a region of rolling countryside dotted with rock outcroppings. There were patches of woodland, few at first, but thicker ahead. They finally came to a shallow stream flowing down from the high country ahead.

"Let's take a breather," Horton said as they caught their breath.

K'nidMin paused to survey the ground ahead, which was rising steadily. "Good idea. We could all use a rest."

R'nemReth shucked her straddle pack with a groan, and settled on her side, too weary to care about the wet underbrush. "How are you doing?" K'nidMin asked her.

"Tired." She was stiff and footsore from the long walk, even at their relaxed pace. From how the civilians, Ic'nichi and human both, collapsed with a chorus of groans and grumbling, she wasn't the only one.

"You're doing good. We're all tired." He offered an encouraging smile, which didn't help much. "We'll get some rest, and take it slower from here."

"How much further will we go?"

K'nidMin pondered that. "I'm not sure. As far as we have to, I guess." After a bit, he added, "We'll keep going until dark, if we don't hit rough ground. If we haven't made contact by then, we'll camp overnight and head back in the morning." He dug in his straddle pack, and offered her a number 4 endurance ration. "Have something to eat. You'll feel better."

"Thank you, I guess, but I have my own." She struggled to her feet, dug through her straddle pack, and came up with some protean bars, some human carrots, and a leftover pastry from first-meal.

Horton laughed out loud at his chagrin. "Way to go, girl friend!"

"Hmmm... Well done," he muttered.

A meal did help, especially since K'nidMin redeemed himself by coming up with a jar of powdered *V'liz*, which he mixed with water from the creek. It was cold, and not the best, but welcome nonetheless. R'nemReth idled over her pastry, enjoying the break, and wondered about K'nidMin. This latest matter with the rations was part of a worrisome trend. Why take the vile endurance rations when there was plenty of real food? For that matter, there was the stiff pace he set, seemingly ignoring the civilians in the herd, many of whom were elderly. It all pointed to a lack of attention to detail. It left her wondering if he knew what he was doing?

She shook the thought off as nonsense: K'nidMin was an experienced Defender, hand picked for this assignment; of course he was competent. She reflected on it for a time, and realized even the best leaders were imperfect. So he overlooked small details now and then; he still ran a tight herd which got things done, even with the humans in the mix. It made him seem more natural somehow. In a way, his small oversights reassured her: he was focussed on bigger things.

§

After resting for a while, they struggled to their feet and moved on. The pace was slower partly because everyone was tired, and partly because the going was more difficult. The day began to wain and the temperature dropped as the breeze picked up. Clouds were coming in from the coast, and the sky looked decidedly unfriendly.

They eventually came to a long, low ridge which angled gently upward toward the distant mountains. By unspoken agreement, they followed that ridge as it climbed toward the high ground in the distance. Some time later, they started getting results.

"Flyer," someone said. There was a lone figure soaring over the foothills in the distance ahead.

"Form a circle!" K'nidMin snapped. "Everyone be quiet!" The military moved out to form a rough picket line around R'nemReth and the civilians.

"Weapons?" Horton called from her position in the circle.

"No! Just keep alert. We don't want to make any overt sign of aggression." K'nidMin turned to R'nemReth. "Alright, now's your chance. Stay calm, stay focussed, and reach out to him."

"I'm not sure I can reach that far."

He gave her arm a reassuring squeeze. "Try."

84

She turned her attention to the distant figure, and began to receive impressions...

§

...The changing seasons at this time of year meant the high passes were often cloud-shrouded and windy. Even here, in the foothills, the winds were roiled by the distant mountains so he had to be constantly alert. Truth, the currents were treacherous as he soared along the low ridge, eyes focussed to a medium search as he scoured the rocks and ledges for evidence of a hideous crime. Such things were rare any more, thankfully, but if he is to be a Seeker, he must be prepared for the worst impulses of the Immaterial in them all. He was prepared to confront a lot in his chosen Calling...but this... It conflicted him, leaving him less than eager to find the crime scene first...

§

"He's an apprentice," R'nemReth said. "Something about finding evidence of a crime."

'Law enforcement: good,' K'nidMin thought. *'He won't attack without reason, then.'*

'You hope,' Hudson thought.

'Aye, an' he's a small 'un,' Sergeant MacIntosh mused. *'Just a wee laddie. He'll no be that hard t' fend off.'*

'Can that sort of thinking!'

R'nemReth tried to ignore the chatter and concentrated on reaching out to the Flyer, but she couldn't help being apprehensive. That 'wee laddie' was enormous. *'Please talk with us,'* she thought...

§

...He longed to be a Seeker since his earliest years, but now that he was confronting the dreadful possibilities, he was riven with doubt. The high winds buffeted him, forcing him toward the forest speeding past, and he banked easily to give himself a bit more room. This was what he always dreamed it would be since he took his first unsteady flight; soaring on the currents on an urgent quest for the Right and True. He always felt free on the wing, and the rush of

85

excitement as he dared the menacing sky helped him put aside his uneasiness for the time. Hopefully, once he received his adult Calling, he would find time for this; to soar on the wind, free of any care or purpose. Flight for its own sake...

§

"He is searching for something." R'nemReth was torn between providing a running commentary and maintaining her link to the distant Flyer. "He's not just out hunting." She was slightly giddy from sharing his joy as he drifted over the landscape. Flying was a new and novel experience for her, even witnessed second-hand.

'What is his mood?' Horton asked.

That strained her concentration. *'He's apprehensive about finding what he's looking for, but really pleased to be flying. He's in a good mood overall.'*

'Excellent. Stay focussed.'

'Easier said than done with all these distractions!'

§

...He swept past the edge of the forest, brushing his wingtip on a scraggly bush, and caught a glimpse of white which brought him back to the here-and-now. He looked closer, but it was nothing, which was a relief in a way. To be a Seeker was a noble Calling, one he felt he would be good at, but some crimes were bad enough to make him doubt he had the wings for such justice. But he was not a Seeker yet; merely a Second-Wing (albeit a promising one he was told). This exercise flight today would put his skills to the test, honing them for the role ahead...

...something... His eye caught a trace of movement below and to his right. He swerved higher to get a good view, and focussed his vision for a long range look...

§

"He sees us." In the distance, the Flyer rose abruptly and turned toward them, clearly studying them. R'nemReth felt his mind, reached out to him, and got a fleeting image of the two of them standing in the open with their herd around them. "His vision is incredible! He can see us in detail."

"Reach out to him!" K'nidMin hissed, breaking her gestalt with the creature.

§

...he circled them warily. There were several figures below, both the tall First Sky-Fallers and the short Second Sky-Fallers. He was a surprised and a bit worried that they left their Aerie and were standing right out in the open, something they never did since their first appearance. He started to turn away...

'Don't go,' a thought came to him. He faltered in surprise, wondering where that notion came from. 'We need to talk,' the thought came again. It was only then he realized the creatures were reaching out to him in some unexpected way...

§

"I'm not sure I'm getting to him," she said as the Flyer circled them warily.

"You are. Did you see how he faltered?"

§

...High overhead, the Flyer studied them in confusion, trying to understand what was happening. Two of the Second Sky-Fallers stood in the middle of the others, looking up at him. 'What do you call yourself?' a thought came to him.

He had no idea of what to make of that, but he got the impression those alien thoughts came from one of the two. He shifted his path to circle them more closely.

'I am called R'nemReth,' another thought came. 'Who are you?'

This changed things. He had no idea what a 'R'nemReth' was, but if the creature bore a Calling, honor demanded he answer. 'I am Young-Seeker', he thought.

'I am pleased to meet you, Young-Seeker. Can we talk for a while? It is important.'

Again, he was confused. The Sky-Fallers showed claws to the Aerie, yet here they were asking to speak as if wing-joined. This was not the Way of the Aeries...but the presence of these creatures and their ability to speak without words cast all the Gathered Truths in doubt. He circled lower, wondering what to do.

'Please help us make peace with your people,' the thought came. 'We want to correct a wrong done to you.'

This perplexed him further. It seemed the Sky-Fallers gave voice...gave something...to acknowledge their breach of Law. They wanted to speak, something one never did with those who extend claws. And they gave...voice...to their wrong-doing. Did they seek to retract claws? Could such a thing be done without the bloodletting? There were so many odd things about these Sky-Fallers, their presence here, and their spirit-words...the Gathered Truths offered no answer. What to do?

He circled them, studying them closely. The larger flight hovered in a circle while the two Second Sky-Fallers, the ones who spoke without speaking, stood alone in the middle. Their position invited attack; it made no sense unless they were prepared to risk death to make their point. Curious, he circled lower...

§

Their circular formation dissolved as the creature swept in just above ground level, backwinged abruptly, and settled a short distance away. "Everyone stay calm!" Horton said. It took some doing, but they managed not to grab their weapons. They reformed in a broad front facing the visitor, everyone nervous but under control for the moment.

"Alright, R'nemReth," K'nidMin said, softly. "Time to do your thing."

She edged forward reluctantly with K'nidMin a pace behind her until they were half way to the Flyer. Up close he was enormous: his wings draped across the ground like a low rise. His head was massive, with a broad mouth filled with sharp carnivorous teeth. There were fleshy stalks on either side of the mouth, tipped with large eyes focussed on them. The massive head was linked to the streamlined body with only a hint of a neck. This was clearly a top predator.

And he was still a youngling, partly grown...

K'nidMin nudged her, which shook her out of her trance. Time to get it done. *'I am R'nemReth,'* she thought. *'We come to speak with your people. We wish to be your friends.'*

The creature pondered them for a time, clearly confused by this exchange. Then he emitted a warbling shriek. *'I do not hear your words, but I do,'* his thought came at the same time. *'How can this be?'*

'I have the gift of speaking directly to your mind. With this gift, we can speak in a common language. Words are not needed.'

She felt a rush of confusion. *'This is strange weather. You do not fly, but your minds do. This is not the Way Of The Aeries.'*

She sensed the emphasis on that last statement. *'Our Aeries are beyond the sky; we have our ways just as you have yours. The first meeting was a tragedy. We come to speak with your leaders to set it right.'*

The visitor pondered them, tilting his enormous head back and forth. She felt a rising tide of suspicion and mistrust. *'Three of the wings have lost their Light. Four more are hurt; one may soon lose her Light as well. How can you offer to align with the Aerie when you extend claws to us?'*

'It was a tragic mistake! We are not your enemies. We hope to make peace with you.'

The creature studied them for a long moment, tilting his massive head from side to side as he did. *'The Gray-Wing must hear of this,'* his thought came at last. With that, he lifted into the air with a mighty thrashing of his wings, sending a storm of dust and plant debris swirling around them.

"Well," K'nidMin muttered as they watched the creature fly away. "This is promising."

*****

"Best Laid Plans"

It turned out the weather forecasts were wrong. It was already sprinkling when they returned late in the second day, and by time they gave their report night had fallen and with it a steady drizzle.

"For once I am pleased to admit I was wrong," Arbiter G'nemBrik said after they related their success to the leadership herd. "It's good to see you all made it back unharmed."

Captain Pencroft was less enthusiastic. "Are they planning to attack us? Did you learn anything when you read his mind?"

"That's not what we went out there for!" Learnéd Z'gehRoo protested.

"Still, she was in mental contact, which was our first chance to gain real intelligence on them." He turned to R'nemReth. "Did you receive any impressions about their policies? Do they pose a threat to us?"

There was an uncomfortable silence as the Contact Herd members looked to each other for direction. *'His...thoughts were ill-disposed toward us at first,'* she thought, finally. *'I got the impression they've presumed we're hostile.'*

"This is consistent with a hunting pack culture," Doctor Lassiter noted. "Their mindset will be purely territorial. We've already seen evidence of pack mentality in their hunts."

"Which means there's no reasoning with them!" Pencroft turned on Horton. "You took a *stupid* risk leaving your weapons behind! I am *very* disappointed in your conduct, *Lieutenant!*"

"We did what it took and we got results!" Horton wasn't ready to give him the time of day. "And they aren't mindless animals! They may be predators, but we were able to reason with that one Flyer. He said he would pass the word on to his elders."

'And he changed his mind once I talked with him,' R'nemReth added. *'He was confused by my peace offerings. Maybe they just never thought about talking with us before.'*

"That would follow since we are their first alien contacts," Learnéd C'venBren said.

Pencroft shuddered. "I *hate* this telepathy!" he snapped at R'nemReth. Can't you learn our language like everyone else?"

'Why bother?' she thought back, bluntly. *'You wouldn't listen anyway!'*

K'nidMin stepped in to cool the rising tension. "The important thing is that we made a communication breakthrough. This is our first solid progress since we came here."

"But what exactly have you accomplished?" Sir Miles asked. "You spoke briefly with one native, a young one at that. This hardly sounds like a breakthrough."

"You got that right!" Pencroft snapped.

"It is, sir. Now their elders know we want to talk with them; that we want to make peace. That's half the battle. It's not a final treaty, but at least things are moving."

"We have process now," G'nemBrik rebuked the two humans. "We must build on this beginning."

"And we can thank the Contact Herd for this opportunity," First Degree E'zemBron added to Pencroft. "Especially R'nemReth. Her talent proved to be the wedge we needed." That pleased her no end, adding to her satisfaction at having accomplished the mission.

"Well, I'll be blessed if I can see it," Sir Miles said, doubtfully. "It would seem your whole affair was for nothing."

"That's the fact!" Pencroft said with a contemptuous snort. "They wasted a real chance to learn about the enemy's intentions while chasing after pie-in-the-sky. That's no more than we can be expected with these people, *or* from this so-called 'talent'!" He dismissed R'nemReth, and turned on Horton. "Your performance will figure *prominently* in my report on this expedition, *Lieutenant!*"

§

R'nemReth was right behind Lieutenant Horton when they exited the Admin grotto, and Horton's aura matched her own smoldering, barely suppressed rage. *'What is wrong with those two?'* she fumed.

Horton paused and gave her an angry look. "You better not get me started on them!"

That seemed like good advice, so R'nemReth changed the subject. *'Will you be alright?'*

Horton was angry enough to bite heads off, but her temper was directed elsewhere. "Aside from being under *his* command, I'm fine, thank you."

R'nemReth's temper cooled as her concern for one of her few friends arose. *'You won't get in trouble with your government, will you?'*

Horton sagged and stared wearily at the dripping rain as her temper drifted on the chill breeze. "We're an independent unit," she said at last. "Special forces like us get a lot more leeway than the line apes." She fumed for a bit, then gave R'nemReth a reassuring smile. "And Pencroft is not exactly a stellar officer. I know his reputation. I'll be alright."

Horton pulled her rain tunic tighter and trotted into the night toward the cafeteria just as K'nidMin came by. "You did good in there," he offered.

She sighed at the memory of their thoughts, which left her feeling icky. "What is it with those two humans, anyway? So the Flyers are predators; we knew that all along. Why all the *r'vebbe*?"

"You don't know much about humans, do you? They are pack-hunting predators too, which is why we've been so concerned about them since First Contact. Z'gehRoo would probably say something about them mentally projecting onto the Flyers, which would explain their paranoia."

"I...didn't know that." R'nemReth was a bit dismayed to learn the humans' dark secret, even in her friend Horton. "So why did Pencroft dump on her?"

"Because he can." K'nidMin's ears twitched philosophically. "He was venting his frustrations, and she was a convenient target. Our people do it too. It's the price we pay for being at the back of the herd."

That hardly seemed fair, but she knew it was all too true. "I hope most of the humans are like Horton, then maybe there's a chance for them."

"Maybe. *If* most are like Horton." He pulled his overtunic tighter and nodded toward the cafeteria. "Enough human *x'mnnb'*. Let's get some hot *V'liz*."

§

If anyone expected an immediate breakthrough, they were disappointed. The weather turned raw and blustery with occasional showers over the next couple days. People went about their routines and kept an eager (or anxious) eye to the sky, but there was no sign of the Flyers.

"Where are they?" Horton grumbled as they scanned the horizon from an observation post on the roof of the Admin grotto.

"I hope that youngling we contacted reported in," K'nidMin said. He pulled his overtunic tighter as the sprinkle picked up. "Hopefully he didn't dismiss us altogether."

"Tis a raw day t' be on the wing, sir," Sergeant MacIntosh said. "I'll wager they're home a-bed like any sensible soul."

K'nidMin sighed. "As I would be if I wasn't *n'bna'nmn*."

"There's one!" someone shouted.

They all crowded up to the railing, binoculars at the ready. A lone Flyer could be seen in the distance, drifting high over the prairie.

"It looks like its eyes are turned toward us, sir." A'vemDrem was busy with his telephoto lens as usual.

"You have the best view of any of us. Can you see any unusual detail?"

A'vemDrem rested the bulky lens on the railing and squinted through his viewfinder as he tweaked the controls. "I'd say his head is turned toward us, sir. As much as they can turn their heads anyway. His right eye is definitely looking at us."

"If they're like most flying predators, he'll be able to see us clearly even at this distance," Learnéd C'venBren said.

"Everyone wave to him," Horton ordered. Most of them on the platform solemnly waved their arms at the distant figure. The Flyer ignored them, but continued to drift on the currents in a broad circle around Fort Zinderneuf until it completed its inspection and turned away into the mountains.

After the creature vanished into the mists, they retreated under the overhanging shelter and clustered around a portable gas-fired cooker. "Ancestors," K'nidMin muttered as he poured a bowl of steaming *V'liz*. "I will be thankful to finish this assignment and get back home where I can be dry."

"You and me both." Horton wrapped a thermal blanket around her shoulders and treasured a mug of the humans' 'coffee'. "I'd settle for being back at Checkpoint."

"Who wouldn't?"

"So what do we make of that performance?" K'nidMin's Worthy asked with a nod toward the distant mountains.

"It looked to me like he was checking us out from a distance," K'nidMin said. "They always seemed to just give us a passing once-over when they were out on their hunts before. Now they seem to be taking us seriously."

"Will they come?" Horton asked. "Why are they waiting?"

"They'll come. They wouldn't be reconnoitering otherwise." He pondered for a bit. "They're being cautious, I guess. They don't know the range of our weapons, and they only have our word about our good wishes. They're trying to scope out our intentions."

"Aye, sir. Yon beasties are sizing us up, forby!"

"At least we're getting a reaction," Horton said. "It's something."

The wind picked up, causing all of them to cower in their various blankets. "I hate this," K'nidMin griped. "We're constantly overheating from this cold weather, and I understand you humans are suffering as well."

"That's the truth," Horton sighed. She rubbed her hands and scooted closer to the heater to capture its meager output. "It goes with the territory. This is why we get the big money."

K'nidMin shorted derisively. "Still, this is one of the downsides of military life." He gingerly hefted one of the percolators off the heater and poured another steaming bowl of *V'liz*. "Ancestors, sometimes this is all that keeps me going."

"Then perhaps ye could use a wee r-r-reinforcement, sir." Sargent MacIntosh dug in his kit, came up with a bottle, and offered it to K'nidMin, who reluctantly let him pour a shot into his bowl. "Strictly under the table, ye understand, as it's nae permitted under r-r-regulations."

Lieutenant Horton watched curiously, then extended her coffee mug and received a shot in turn.

§

R'nemReth wasn't on the observation deck since she had the sense to come in out of the rain, but she was heartened to hear the Flyers were responding to her invitation, however reluctantly. She was in the cafeteria at the moment enjoying a meal of *uf'thoka,* and the news of their visitor lifted a load of worry off her back.

The last few days were frustrating, and the lack of response from the Flyers thus far put a damper on her sense of accomplishment. There was still a long way to go before a formal peace was established, and she was eager to get on with it. But now things were moving. This appearance suggested that the end of her mission was finally coming into view.

She tried to help by reaching out with her mind to the distant Flyer, but if he heard her, he didn't respond.

§

The leadership met the next morning to plan the next step now that the Flyers were responding. R'nemReth was part of the discussion since she would serve as translator, although she mostly received instructions rather than offering input. Still, being part of something this important thrilled her, and she eagerly followed the arcane process of interstellar diplomacy.

The conversation soon drifted to military matters however, which soon turned into an argument over their defenses, goaded on by Captain Pencroft and Sir Miles.

"This is *er'trxxda!*" E'zemBron complained. "This is already an armed camp, and there's not much improvement you can made to our perimeter. This *r'vebbe* over a possible attack is *cc'v'renk!*"

"And it can't make a good impression on the Flyers, who we are trying to coax to the peace table," Arbiter G'nemBrik said.

"*You* may be willing to risk lives, but I am *not!*" Pencroft shouted. "Better safe than sorry! Everyone keeps busy on our defenses until we *know* we can turn our backs on those monsters, if ever!"

"And if the effort proves unnecessary, then no harm done," Sir Miles added.

Neither Horton nor the Ic'nichi shared his optimistic belief, but there was no arguing it, try as they would. The meeting broke up on a sour note.

Captain Pencroft's idea of 'keeping everyone busy' had the human garrison going through the motions in the chill rain, which caused no end of griping. Aside from stringing the last of the barbed wire, tidying up the sandbag emplacements and distributing more ammunition to forward positions, there was little to be done. They simply didn't have the materials, so the humans made busy-work and grumbled.

First Degree E'zemBron had no sympathy with the Captain's foolishness, and ordered the Ic'nichi to remain indoors. This caused complaints in the Admin grotto, weary envy from the much-abused human garrison, and quiet gratitude among the four hands' worth of 'Dark Grays' ground forces.

Captain Pencroft soon picked up on the grumbling, and tried to motivate his people by lambasting them with scare talk about a possible Flyer attack. The human peacekeepers listened in silence, then went on with their work with no greater enthusiasm than before. Their efforts didn't improve, and their workmanship suffered.

The Ic'nichi watched all this and worried about his effect on the peacekeepers' morale, which was clearly faltering. Life went on.

§

On the third day the weather improved and the Flyers were back in force. A hands' worth circled over the camp at a distance, no doubt checking them out further. The humans stopped work and manned the defenses while the joint Contact Herd gathered on an observation platform.

'Welcome,' R'nemReth thought to them from their vantage point. *'Please come down. We want to talk with you.'* If they heard her, they ignored the invitation, but continued to circle for a while before flying away.

"They're sizing us up," Captain Pencroft grumbled when the administrators met a short while later. "They *must* be planning to attack us."

"You don't know that," E'zemBron said. "They're simply being cautious, is all."

"It makes perfect sense! Why put up with us here when they could simply wipe us out?"

"Spoken like the proud megalomaniac!" Doctor Lassiter said, scornfully. "Primitive cultures can't afford to waste lives as cannon fodder, especially against advanced foes. They usually don't risk general warfare if they can avoid it."

"Especially after the firepower they met from the original landing party," Lieutenant Horton said, pointedly. Pencroft gave her a sharp glare, but said nothing.

§

The defenses work never did amount to much, and the morale of the human peacekeepers soon lagged, as did their efforts. Pencroft called them all into ranks, in the rain, and lectured them at length about the Flyer 'threat', which produced nothing more than further grumbling.

"How are they taking it?" K'nidMin asked as they watched from a discreet distance.

R'nemReth focussed on the human ranks, and what she felt was disquieting. "They're scared. They're angry. They're frustrated. He's working them up into a fine state."

She felt K'nidMin's dismay as he stood next to her. "Great. Anything could happen."

§

"Why haven't they returned?" Sir Miles asked two days later.

"It could be they have the sense to come in out of the rain," E'zemBron grumbled. The last Flyer appearance turned out to be a brief interlude between rain storms. "They must know the weather here better than we ever will, so you need to be patient."

"Be thankful for this lousy weather," Pencroft said, sternly. "We can use the time to improve our defenses."

"This is ridiculous!" Horton complained. "You're working our people to exhaustion, and all this talk about a Flyer attack has them spooked."

"That will be ENOUGH, *Lieutenant!*" Pencroft yelled. "I will determine what threats we face, and I want our people *properly* prepared to meet it!"

"We've sensed rising tension approaching paranoia in your people," K'nidMin said. "Your force is on edge; something could break."

"I agree," E'zemBron said. "You're pushing your people too hard over a purely fanciful threat. This isn't healthy for morale or discipline."

Pencroft gave him a sizzling glare. "You let me worry about our people! We're a lot tougher than you lizards, and if you'd get off your dead asses and do your part, we'd all be a lot better off!"

"That is uncalled for!" Arbiter G'nemBrik complained.

"Indeed, Captain," Sir Miles said, loftily. "Let's not allow our differences to run riot."

Pencroft bit back on his temper. "None the less, Ambassador, it is foolish to assume they won't attack us."

"*Of course* they won't attack us!" E'zemBron said. "Why should they, now that they know we want to talk? And if they were going to, they would have by now."

§

"I'm sorry about that cheap crack," Horton said to them after the meeting broke up. "Some of us just don't want to accept you since you are too different."

"It's understandable," K'nidMin said, philosophically. "We know your people are afraid of us. They train us to be circumspect around you to avoid antagonisms."

"There's no excuse for trash-talking you like that!"

"We don't take it personally." In fact R'nemReth did take his 'lizard' remark as deeply insulting, but K'nidMin's example helped her put it behind her. "I am concerned about your peoples' morale," he added.

Horton gave him a frustrated look. "You're not the only one. That idiot Pencroft has them in a lather with all his *gotterdammerung* crap. That's not the way to inspire troops!"

"It certainly doesn't seem so. I was under the impression your leadership training was better than this."

"You would think!" She fought to contain her temper. "He's a mediocre son and grandson of somebody; a staff toady. He's up to his...brass...in the Old Boy Network, and so is Sir Miles. There's no other explanation for how they got this far."

K'nidMin offered a humorless snort. "One thing we have in common, anyway: the dregs gravitate to the staff."

"What frightens me is Pencroft hopes to get a promotion out of this. I hear he might be quota'd out if he doesn't improve. He needs a big win, and he'll likely settle for a military win."

K'nidMin nodded. "Scale polishing; I might have guessed. That *s'vem'grott n'bna'nmn* could push to the point where something breaks in his desperation."

"Then he gets himself a big battle so he can come out smelling like a hero!" Horton pounded the railing in frustration. "I swear shame itself curled up and died when those two were appointed to this project!"

§

The next day brought dramatic developments. The sky cleared, allowing a weak daylight through scattered clouds. It was perfect flying weather, by local standards anyway, and the Flyers arrived in force. A solid two hands of them appeared in mid morning, sending the humans scrambling to their gun positions while the Ic'nichi mostly took to the observation posts to watch the proceedings.

"This is it," Horton said. They've come to talk."

"Are you sure?" R'nemReth asked. The sight of all those enormous Flyers closing on them was a bit unnerving.

Horton gave her a reassuring smile. "There's not enough of them for a serious attack."

"And a primitive culture wouldn't waste useful lives on foolish gestures," Learnéd C'venBren added.

"Those are probably their tribal elders," Doctor Lassiter said as they watched the circling host. "I'd say they're finally ready to talk with us."

"Ready to hear what we have to say, anyway," C'venBren said. "We still have to sell them on our good intentions."

"That's the diplomats' problem," Horton said. "We did our part. Now it's up to the brains to settle things." The excitement was building as their moment of triumph approached.

K'nidMin turned to R'nemReth. "Can you hear anything from them? Can you detect their thoughts?"

"I'll try," she said, uncertainly. She stared at the approaching Flyers, cleared her mind, and reached out to them. *'I can sense them,'* she thought so the humans could listen. *'It's hard to tell...they are curious...confused...'* She pondered the alien sensations for a long moment. *'They seem...I think they want to learn more about us. They don't know what to make of us.'*

"That would follow your original contact," Doctor Lassiter said. "They don't seem to be in the habit of negotiating. We must confound them."

"This sounds hopeful," K'nidMin said. "If they'll listen, we can clear up all the misunderstandings."

"That's how it usually works," Doctor Lassiter said. "*IF* both sides are willing to listen."

The Flyers circled the encampment, easing lower as they did. An historic meeting was moments away.

"Are we ready?" Horton asked.

"We are. We can only hope G'nemBrik and Sir Miles aren't off chasing their own tails." It was hard to be pessimistic in the excitement of the hour.

"There they are now." K'nidMin pointed to the two diplomats who were headed for the main gate. "We're watching history being made!"

The Flyers circled the encampment cautiously, easing lower, lining up to land just beyond the barbed wire perimeter...

...They were startled by a sudden noise, and the air was lit up with bright streaks of tracers: one of the humans had opened up with a machine gun!

They looked around in confusion trying to figure out what was going on, then Horton yelled, "Cease fire!" as she sprinted toward the gun position over the adjacent rooftops, yelling at the top of her lungs. "Cease fire, you idiots!"

The gun fired one more burst then quit abruptly, but the damage was done. The Flyers swerved away from the spray of tracers and beat a hasty retreat.

"*p'quas'tka!*" K'nidMin groaned in dismay. "Those *n'bna'nmn* humans may have just wrecked any hope of solving this mess!"

*****

"Picking Up The Pieces"

"I *swear* I'll have that idiot court-marshaled!" Horton was still livid after the panic subsided. "I'll have him broken and drummed out!" She was pacing back and forth in frustration, her snout a mask of rage and bitterness.

R'nemReth was stunned by how fast things fell apart, by how swiftly her high hopes were shattered. "What happened?" she muttered to K'nidMin.

He offered a vexed ear twitch. "I told you: the humans are homicidal *er'trxxda*," he said, softly. "I think you can see the problem now."

"He...seemed more like he was panicked," she whispered.

K'nidMin gave her a searching look. "You felt that? You can thank Captain Pencroft for getting them worked up. Even so, they're all unstable. We should have anticipated something like this and taken precautions."

Horton noticed them whispering among themselves and broke off her rant. "How bad is it?"

"I don't see how it could get much worse," K'nidMin told her, somberly. "At least none of them were hit, I hope. But I'd say all our progress to date just got stampeded."

"I'm so sorry!"

"It's not your fault. One of your people panicked."

"I *wish* we had more say about who gets assigned here!" Horton's frustration was boiling over to where it started affecting R'nemReth. "They don't listen to us line apes. As far as Geneva cares, as long as someone is aggressive and follows orders, that's all they want!"

'Your leaders aren't too picky, are they?' R'nemReth thought as *her* frustration boiled over in turn.

'R'nemReth...' K'nidMin cautioned her.

Horton glared at her, then her anger subsided a bit. "We can't afford to be," she muttered.

"She is on our side," K'nidMin scolded her after Horton left. "She can't help what happened, so there's no sense in knotting her tail over it."

R'nemReth fumed for a bit, then backed down. "Sorry. So what do we do now?"

He sighed in frustration. "I wish I knew."

§

"Is there *any* way we can salvage this mess?" Arbiter G'nemBrik pleaded when the leadership met again.

"Honestly, sir...probably not," K'nidMin said. "They must think our original contact was an attempt to lure them in."

"And we fired on their tribal elders, too." Horton was still fuming over what happened earlier. "They'll assume we tried to assassinate their leadership!"

The Administrative circle were pensive and depressed by how bad things had become. "Well that does it," Sir Miles said. "There's no hope of establishing relations with them now."

"Right now we need to worry about an attack," Captain Pencroft said. "We run a very real risk of retaliation."

"Thanks to the *p'quas'tka* of *your* people!" First Degree E'zemBron snarled. "Your peoples' lack of discipline is *cc'v'renk!* I would turn in my placard before I would command such *n'bna'nmn!*"

"Which doesn't say much for the fighting qualities of your troops, or *you!*"

"ENOUGH!" Arbiter G'nemBrik shouted. "We face a crisis, and this is no time for recriminations!" The others quieted down, and the mood in the room turned to quiet desperation.

"If they do attack, can we resist them?" Sir Miles asked.

"We can strengthen our positions some more," Pencroft said, grimly. "We don't have all that much ammunition, but if we give them a bloodying the first time, they'll hesitate to come back."

"How soon can we evacuate?"

"The 'Comanche' isn't due back for another week. And even then, it would take at least a month to scare up a colony transport to evacuate us. Assuming one is available."

"What about the Ic'nichi?"

Pencroft bit back a sharp remark. "They would have to get word back home via Checkpoint, and then diplomatic clearances would be needed for one of their ships to come into our space."

Sir Miles nodded in resignation. "Months, then. I don't suppose we can evacuate them, at least to Checkpoint?"

"I doubt if we can scrape up a second transport any sooner than they could send one of theirs."

"So what do we do?"

"There's only one thing we can do," Pencroft said. "Hunker down and withstand a siege until help arrives."

§

The next day was uneventful, not that it helped the general sense of gloom. The orbital weather satellite showed another storm front building up over the ocean, and the base meteorologist predicted rain over the next several days. Clouds rolled in from the sea. The temperature dropped, and there were occasional showers.

Recriminations ran high between the Ic'nichi and the humans. Arbiter G'nemBrik and Sir Miles argued bitterly over who was at fault; the upshot being the human who opened fire was relieved of duty and earmarked to be sent home, but would not be court-marshaled, to Lieutenant Horton's disgust.

This did nothing to relieve tensions goaded on by the miserable, wet weather. There were a few fights, though thankfully no one was injured. Both Ic'nichi and humans were put on report. Morale and discipline suffered in both camps. Fort Zinderneuf became a sinkhole of bitterness and frustration.

As for R'nemReth, she remained in her quarters, trying to shut out a world which betrayed her once again. Her anger turned to despair, and she felt tempted to end it all rather than face the future waiting on d'enchia... She shut the thought firmly out of her mind. She was a survivor: she wouldn't let the Universe beat her, although what she could do now was beyond her. She pulled the cover up over her head and tried not to think about tomorrow, or failure, or her flirtation with self destruction.

§

"Our morale is in the dumper." Lieutenant Horton and K'nidMin were about the only informal line of communications still running, and both put major efforts into keeping the peace. "It looks like our people are ready to give up."

103

The two met in a quiet corner of the base commissary along with Sergeant MacIntosh and K'nidMin's Worthy. Aside from the kitchen staff they pretty well had the place to themselves since it was pouring rain at the moment and a stiff wind filled the air with salt spray from the nearby beach. Aside from those unlucky souls on guard duty, most of the combined force chose to remain in quarters.

"We're not much better off," K'nidMin said. "Most of our people feel it's hopeless." He took another sip of *V'liz*. "Many of ours feel this herd can't do anything right."

"As with ours too, sir," MacIntosh said. "This beastly weather does na' help, either. We need a victory t' pick up the spirits in the ranks all r-r-round."

Horton nodded grimly. "The only one happy right now is Pencroft. It's starting to look like he'll get his *gotterdammerung* battle after all."

"Aye. And that will'na be a bonny sight, forby!"

"I wonder..." K'nidMin was struck with an ugly thought.

Horton eyed him curiously. "What?"

"Do you think...Pencroft might have set us up? You said he wants an heroic battle..."

The tension amped in their circle. "God," Horton muttered. "If he did..."

"He'd be court-marshaled and drummed out if that er came t' light!" MacIntosh swore.

Horton pondered the thought, then shook her head. "He's not brave enough to risk it, nor smart enough, either."

They were able to breathe easier. "What really bothers me is that the whole First Contact program could fall apart. We're *needed* out here!"

"You got that right!" Horton said. "What scares me is we may wind up having to contact a star-traveling race with this Fuster Cluck! As is, we could do more harm than good."

"We *have* to make this work," K'nidMin said, grimly.

"Yeah. But how? I doubt the 'brains' will let us leave the compound again."

"That might na' be wise in any event, sir," MacIntosh added.

There was an uncomfortable silence as the leaders pondered their options. "The trouble is the established doctrine we were handed isn't working," K'nidMin said at last.

"What do you expect from the swivel-chair hussars?" Horton said, bitterly. "They're safe and comfortable sitting on their...rear echelons...while we have to make their pipe-dreams work!"

"Oy! Truer words were never spoken. But without doctrine, what can we do?"

"We *invent* doctrine! If necessity is the mother of invention, raw survival is one hell of a midwife."

K'nidMin chuckled humorlessly. "Good one!" Then he turned somber again. "I hope we can find the right 'midwife' in time."

"I heard rumors your special talent has troubles back home," Horton said as they broke up. "I hear she needs this more than any of us."

K'nidMin was candid, if discreet. "She is hoping for a fresh start. It doesn't look like that will happen now."

Horton sighed. "That's a shame. She seems like a nice kid."

§

R'nemReth was resting in her quarters, but overhearing her mentioned snapped her out of a withdrawn funk. *'She comes from a troubled background,'* K'nidMin's words echoed in her thoughts. *'It's a shame; she has real potential. I hate the idea of failing for her sake alone.'*

'Well good luck! She's a decent sort who could use a break.'

'She could, indeed.'

She lay on her cot staring at the wall and tried to make sense of their sympathy. She was surprised by how Horton supported her, especially for a human, seeing how temperamental she was. And K'nidMin...she knew he was attracted to her, but she hadn't realized how concerned he was as well, not that what they thought of her would make a difference.

She was still shaken—and increasingly angry—at how fast her hopes for a bright future were dashed. She *hated* those *l'cc'vn* humans, especially the *n'bna'nmn* who wrecked everything in a fit of panic. Thanks to his...*cc'v'renk!*...her fate was sealed. The Ki-Elder would never give her the benefit of the doubt.

The room was chilly, and the steady rain beating on the roof was depressing. She thought about switching on the lamp, but its charge was low since the solar cell on the roof couldn't do much in this dismal weather. It symbolized the whole sorry, soggy mess; the sorry state of her life in general. But there was nothing to do but bear up, as usual. She pulled the blanket up around her head and tried to tune the world out again. She had a lot to think about.

§

The leaders called the joint Contact Herd together that afternoon, and they argued at length over what, if anything, could be done. At times the debate was as hostile as interspecies relations were in general. K'nidMin and Horton cracked down hard when tempers flared, which kept the joint herd from collapsing altogether. About the only thing they agreed on in the end was that the Flyers needed to make the next move. There was little hope they would.

The talks were troubled by rumors spreading rapidly about the effort being written off and the planet evacuated. If that happened, it would not only be a failure for the joint contact project, but could result in them being broken up despite the program being mandated in a treaty between the Ic'nichi and humans. The one thing holding the evacuation back was waiting for the human ship to drop by again on its rounds, and for the humans to summon the transport needed to take them away.

Arbiter G'nemBrik and First Degree E'zemBron fretted mightily over how to hold Fort Zinderneuf with their limited force of 'Dark Grays' once the humans left. They argued fiercely with Sir Miles and Captain Pencroft, complaining that the humans were needlessly putting them at risk unless they either stayed until enough transports arrived, or somehow arranged to evacuate them at the same time. That bought them nothing; not even a concession to leave the human machine guns behind. Tensions between the two races were soon at the breaking point.

As for the Contact Herd, they had a little time, but couldn't afford to waste a moment of it. Sadly, with the way things were just then, wasting time was all they could do. They were hobbled by a flat prohibition against leaving the protection of the compound, and by being completely out of ideas. Unless the Flyers showed up willing to talk—something no one expected by then—the joint Contact Herd was out of business.

R'nemReth and Learnéd Z'gehRoo used the time to work on her psychic training. Unless and until they were evacuated, K'nidMin wanted her to hang on to her telepathic power in case an opportunity came up. She didn't hold out any hope by then, and frankly couldn't care less, but the psychic training also helped her damp down the faint background noise of all the minds around her. With all the angst and bitterness in Fort Zinderneuf, she needed the training for her own mental well-being. In any case, it kept her busy so she didn't have time to brood over her fate. As much as she hated it, she had to admit she was getting fairly good at telepathy.

Days passed. There was no sign of the Flyers. Tensions rose. The humans were hard at work adding to their defensive positions despite the soggy weather, which did their tempers no good. The Ic'nichi garrison weren't as heavily armed, but they kept busy adding to the barricades between buildings and in the central courtyard. A siege mentality pervaded the air, setting R'nemReth's nerves on edge.

"I swear I'm going *er'trxxda!*" she complained to Learnéd Z'gehRoo. "All this anger and tension and...fear...how do the humans stand it?"

"It's how they are," he said, soothingly. "And if its any comfort, all of us feel the tension through our enhanced empathy."

She gave him a hostile glare. "That is *not* comforting!"

He pondered her for a long moment. "If you need, I can prescribe something; a mild anti-depressant perhaps."

That was mortally tempting, but one thing she learned early on the street was always keep a sharp mind. Aside from a bowl of *'sti'eit* on occasion, taking drugs of any sort scared her. "No, thanks," she told him, largely because she dared not dwell on the possibility. "I'll manage."

Her 'zen' lessons continued. The defensive work continued. The tensions between the two races continued with occasional flare-ups. More people were put on report for fighting or

107

insubordination. The rain finally let up after several days, but the chill daylight showing through the cloud cover did little to improve their spirits.

The Flyers' absence continued as well.

§

Four days later, R'nemReth was awakened from an early morning drowse by K'nidMin rapping on her room's door. "They're back!" he said before disappearing at the gallop. The alarm was blaring in the distance, which galvanized her out of her stupor. She struggled into a set of fatigues and trotted after him.

The weather was raw. The humans were scrambling to their gun positions as non-essential staff took shelter in the cafeteria. The 'Dark Grays' garrison were taking position at points between the buildings since they hadn't brought any heavy weapons—another running sore point between species—so were being deployed to guard the perimeter. The combined Ic'nichi-human force was dismayingly thin.

She caught up with K'nidMin and the rest of the Contact Herd on one of the observation platforms. A stiff wind drove a light sprinkle into her eyes, forcing her to shade them with her arm to see the Flyers in the distance. It was another hunt. The herd beasts were near panic as the Flyers swooped down on them, driving them into a compact, churning mass. As before, four Flyers formed a picket line while the rest set up the hunt.

"It's brilliant." Specialist A'vemDrem was busy with his enormous telephoto lens again. "They have a magnificent hunter's instinct." Having witnessed a hunt before, R'nemReth wasn't so thrilled, but said nothing.

They watched in silence for a long moment before K'nidMin made up his mind. "Enough of this!" he snapped. "This is our last chance, so we need to move now!"

"What do you mean?" Learnéd C'venBren asked.

K'nidMin glanced at R'nemReth. "We might still connect with them if we move fast. But we need to gallop if were to get there before their hunt is done."

R'nemReth wasn't thrilled by the energy he radiated. "I don't think I can reach that far," she said.

He gave her an earnest ear twitch. "Then we'll go to them! They're close enough to the encampment that we can stage a fighting retreat if we have to."

"But we're under orders to remain here," his Worthy said.

"To the Uttermost Darkness with orders! We have an opportunity to contact them, but we'll have to hurry."

Learnéd Z'gehRoo held up his arms. "I'll only slow you down. Besides I've already done as much as I can."

"Alright, but if we're going, we need to gallop!" He scrambled for the stairs with R'nemReth a half step behind.

§

Lieutenant Horton turned up as they were sorting themselves out. "You're going out, aren't you?"

"We have one last chance to reconnect, but we'll have to move quickly." K'nidMin gave her a somber ear twitch. "Honestly, if your people come along, it'll make this that much harder. You're supposed to, but..."

"The 'brains' won't buy this."

"Then we won't bother them with petty details!" He buttoned up his overtunic and loosened his sidearm in its holster as the rest of his herd pulled themselves into a rough marching order. "You said the other day about inventing doctrine: one of the keys to success is the unflinching belief that there are no rules."

Horton nodded. "Go get 'em. I'll run interference with the front office." As K'nidMin turned away, she added, "Good luck out there."

§

They had a lengthy gallop to reach the area where the Flyers were hunting. R'nemReth was winded and staggering by time they got there, and Learnéd C'venBren had fallen behind.

"This will do," K'nidMin gasped. They were still a thousand lengths or more from the flying picket line, which was shifting front to bar their way, and none of them wanted to risk going any closer. "Are you in range?" he asked R'nemReth.

"I think so." The distance was less, in fact, than when she first connected with Young-Seeker.

"Alright then, this is your chance!"

The Flyers were well aware of their presence. The picket line drew closer together and moved to partly surround them while the hunting party hurried through their catches. R'nemReth tried hard to reach out to them. *'Please give us a second chance,'* she thought to them. *'One of the humans panicked. It was a mistake. Please talk to us.'* But they didn't respond. One of the Flyers faltered as it flew nearby, but otherwise there was no reply, no sign they heard her or were willing to answer.

"This isn't working," K'nidMin grumbled.

"They don't trust us now," his Worthy added.

"Can you blame them?" C'venBren said.

'Please listen! The humans—the other aliens—were afraid of you. One of them panicked. Please talk to us!'

"I wouldn't trust us either, after what happened yesterday." K'nidMin's aura was dark with pessimism and a rising sense of despair as the hunt progressed until only the picket line was left.

"We have *n'vebRnng* to offer them. This is a wasted effort."

"Can the noise!" she snapped, which shut their grumbling down abruptly. *'Don't go!'* she called to the Flyers. *'We can still salvage this situation!'*

The picket line ignored her as they peeled off one by one to take their catches. *'We don't mean you any harm!'* She watched the last one soar away, then gave K'nidMin a bitter look. "It's ended, isn't it? We failed."

"The humans failed."

"Not that it makes a difference!" The chill breeze left her agitated and edgy. "So what happens to me?"

K'nidMin didn't answer, but stared off into the distance as the Flyers withdrew, his aura churning with regret and indecision. "I...suppose we go back to d'enchia." He turned to her with a somber expression. "This wasn't your fault. I'll talk to the Ki-Elder, explain what happened..."

"That one? He won't lift a *finger* to help me!"

"But...you're his hatchling..."

Her bitterness overflowed. "He's ashamed of me! He'd like nothing more than for me to be shipped off to some *Ancestorless* penal nest so I won't embarrass him any more!"

K'nidMin was silent until her tirade wound down. "I'm sure something can be done. A petition to the court, maybe." His aura said differently. There was only so much a Second Degree could do, especially with the Fleet First dead-set against her.

"For all the good it would do," she muttered bitterly. She could sense the collective angst and despair of the Contact Herd, with the larger aura of the compound in the distance. All of a sudden she just couldn't take any more. "Can we at least get rid of this *x'mnnb'* telepathy? I never wanted it in the first place, and its useless now."

K'nidMin's aura was filled with concern. "We can do that if you want, but please hold off for a while longer. Something may come up to save the situation yet."

"I am so *sick* of hearing about this *l'cc'vn* situation!" The chill breeze picked up, sending a flush of body heat through her. Her angst turned to despair. She turned and started the long trudge back to the encampment. "Enough of this. The system tail-knotted me again. Let's get out of this cold."

*****

"Desperation Time"

K'nidMin found her later that afternoon hiding from the Universe in her quarters with her third bottle of *'sti'eit*. "There you are! I've been looking all over for you."

"Leave me alone!" she sobbed, then broke down crying. The scope of the disaster finally soaked in, crumbling her spirit as surely as if she was hit by that machine gun.

K'nidMin studied her in concern for a moment, then tried to comfort her, but she shook him off and turned away. "I understand how you feel," he said, softly. "It seems like your whole world is falling apart, like your last hope has been taken from you. But diving into a bottle doesn't help. I know."

"I c-can't help it...it's hopeless."

"It's only hopeless if you give up. Look: the situation is bad, there's no denying it. It seems like you're doomed, but we're not licked yet. We still have galloping room, but you need to be strong. Have faith in yourself. We'll find a way."

She pulled herself together enough to face him. "I...I'm sorry...I just couldn't..."

"I know." He gave her a reassuring smile. "But this is not the answer."

That didn't help her self-confidence, which was rocky at best. "You...must think I'm a failure."

"No. We all face a crisis in confidence at one point or another. It happens so often, especially in new recruits, that the 'Dark Grays' plan for it." He took her by one arm and helped her to her feet, then took her snout in both hands. "You aren't a failure. You're simply afraid, overwhelmed by your problems. It feels like the whole Universe is knotting your tail, and there's no hope for you." He nibbled her ear tenderly. "You're mistaken, trust me. Come on, it's time to pick up the pieces."

§

He led her to the cafeteria steadying her by one arm, steered her to a quiet corner away from the few others there, and poured her onto one of the collapsable seat cushions. "Hang on, I'll get you something."

She felt better—or more sober at least—after her third bowl of *V'liz*. "I'm sorry," she mumbled at last. "I don't usually..."

"Don't feel ashamed. We all stumble and fall into a bottle at some point; I have. But now you've gotten past it, so the time has come to pull yourself together and get on with life."

She toyed with the plate of canned *bv'nunma* he put in front of her as she pondered a bleak future. It wasn't the best she'd tasted, and she wasn't really hungry, but having a bite to eat gave her more energy, and his sympathy helped her feel a bit less lost.

"I just don't see any hope," she said, quietly. "The Flyers will never listen to us now, and without them I'll never get that Writ of Forbearance."

"We still have a chance to salvage this mess."

She caught what he was thinking before he could say it. "Are you *er'trxxda*?!" she asked in amazement. "That'll never work!"

"Maybe, maybe not. But we can be sure it *won't* work if we don't try."

"The 'brains' will never approve it," she said, doubtfully.

"Then we won't bother them by asking."

She was shaken by what he was planning, although she could see it was her only chance. "We...could get killed..."

K'nidMin studied her eyes while his aura radiated concern and resolve. "Yes, that could happen. If it does, you won't be any worse off than you are now. I'm willing to bet my life it *won't* happen, because I have faith in you and your abilities."

That both dismayed her and thrilled her at the same time. His faith in her was something she never knew on the street. It made her feel good; it made her feel accepted, even admired. It also saddled her with the burden of his life. His trust in her abilities could lead him to a gristly death, unless she found in herself the strength to rise to the crisis.

It was simple, really: either she could link with the Flyers in a moment of crisis, of confrontation with a race with good reason not to trust them...or she couldn't. If she failed, they would die, and there was no way to know in advance if she *could*. The only thing to do was put their lives on the line, and hope for the best.

"Well..." she mumbled. "...I guess we don't have a choice."

In any case, dying couldn't be any worse than the living death of a life sentence. And C'traBenla, her mother, would no doubt knot the Ki-Elder's tail and collect his ears righteously for sending her to her death, so some good could come of it.

§

Arbiter G'nemBrik was in a foul mood when they called upon him in his quarters. "I swear those humans will be the ruin of us all," he greeted them.

"Likely," K'nidMin said. "But we're not finished yet."

G'nemBrik gave him a hostile look. "I admire your eternal optimism, Second. I only wish I knew your secret."

"The secret is simple enough, sir. We keep trying until we make a breakthrough."

G'nemBrik pondered him for a moment, then sagged onto a folding seat cushion. His already pale complexion seemed sickly in the dim light of the single window and a battery lamp. His quarters were no better than anyone else: bleak, damp and functional, with a small electric heater to fight the chill.

"What breakthrough?" he asked, plaintively. "The natives won't come anywhere near this place now, and I daresay they have become very skittish at the sight of humans in general."

"Then we solve both those problems by taking a bold move: we go to them."

"You tried that already, without success."

"Then we make an even bolder move, sir. If the Flyers won't come to us, we'll go to where they live. They can't ignore us then."

G'nemBrik slumped on the camp table and eyed him in amazement. "You plan to go to their aeries?"

"Up into the foothills anyway, far enough from this settlement that the humans won't pose a problem and the Flyers will know we seriously want to talk with them."

G'nemBrik brooded on that. "You run the risk of being killed, you know. The Flyers may have decided we're a danger to them, and won't be willing to listen."

"It's a chance we have to take, sir."

G'nemBrik studied his snout skeptically, then turned to R'nemReth. "And what do you think of this?"

She wasn't sure what her feelings were beyond anxiety and self-doubt, but by then she had nothing to lose. "It's the only option we have left," she muttered.

He turned back to K'nidMin. "You don't intend to tell the others, do you?"

"What good would it do, sir?" He only decided to tell G'nemBrik in order to maintain some fiction of legality.

The Arbiter sighed. "None." He pondered the two, and R'nemReth could feel his alarm, and indecision, and grudging admiration. "You'll likely wind up being eaten."

"If so it might give you here early warning. If we don't come back, you can assume they plan to attack this place."

G'nemBrik turned pale, and his aura seethed with alarm. "Do you think they will?"

"They're predators, sir. We can't rule the possibility out, which is all the more reason for us to take the gamble. In any case, if we don't make a bold move, this whole effort will have been for nothing."

"But your herd isn't large enough to protect you, and we don't have enough people here to provide an adequate escort."

"Then we go alone, just her and me. We don't want to go into their territory in force anyway. Plus that way the humans won't know until long after we're gone, and what they don't know about they can't interfere with."

G'nemBrik shook his head in dismay. "For sheer *l'fru'ng*, you go a long way. This may be all for nothing. The human ship will be here in another three days..."

"And it will be the end of the year before d'enchia can get a transport here to evacuate us. The humans will probably pull out as soon as their transport arrives, leaving us to fend for ourselves. There's no way we can hold this place by ourselves unless we can make peace with the Flyers."

"Sir Miles and Captain Pencroft knotted my tail righteously over your little adventure this morning, and all for nothing. I'm afraid they'll be impossible after this."

"Unless we succeed, of course." G'nemBrik looked askance at him. "We *are* an independent command, sir."

G'nemBrik sighed, and his aura was bleak with despair. "This is *cc'v'renk*. You two will probably be killed, and the whole joint contact program could be wrecked."

"Maybe. But sheer *cc'v'renk* could impress the Flyers enough to get their attention." There was an uncomfortable silence while G'nemBrik absorbed that. "If we can once get the Flyers talking without trigger-happy *humans* around to muck things up, we can save this mission."

G'nemBrik sagged in his seat cushion, his ears twitching in dismay. "I...guess you're right, Ancestors save us." His battery lamp chose that moment to run down, leaving them in near gloom. "I hate this miserable assignment!" His aura was flooded with angst. Finally he looked up at K'nidMin. "This might be the only way. I just hope you two manage to live through it."

§

"Do you really think they will attack this place?" R'nemReth asked after they left.

"There's no way to tell," K'nidMin said, reluctantly. "But we have to keep it in mind."

"Then going out there could be a suicide mission!"

K'nidMin paused and turned to her. "We can count on you to get through to them. If we can get them talking, we can save the situation and ourselves." He gave her an earnest ear twitch. "I'll do my best to protect you."

She could sense that he was sincerely determined to watch over her, and more than a bit afraid of what could happen out there. "How can you protect me from *them?* You can't carry enough guns to fight them off!"

"R'nemReth...we have to have faith. We have to take a gamble and hope we can make it pay." He caressed her snout somberly. "Sargent MacIntosh once taught me a human saying: 'Though I walk through the valley of the shadow of death, I will fear no evil'. You have to walk through that valley of death if you are ever to win your freedom."

The very idea appalled her. "I'm...afraid..."

"So am I," he said, quietly. "Anyone who isn't afraid in a situation like this is either *hro'n'nad* or *n'bna'nmn* or both." His aura was bleak. "Courage isn't an absence of fear; it is being afraid and doing what you have to anyway. I know you have the strength; trust yourself."

She sighed in resignation, although she knew he was right. His performance with G'nemBrik, his iron-clad certainty once a course of action was decided upon, stiffened her own resolve. As hopeless as it seemed, she had to take the risk. If it failed, she was determined to go down fighting.

"If this isn't the Ultimate Cosmic Tail Knot, I can't imagine what would be," she grumbled.

"Let's hope we never find out."

§

They ran into Lieutenant Horton near the camp commissary, and she seemed troubled. "I'm under orders," she said, reluctantly. "Captain Pencroft got on my case about not going out with you this morning. He ordered me to immediately report if any of your people leave the camp." Her aura was somber and unhappy. "I'm sorry."

"Don't be," K'nidMin said. "You have to follow orders. No one can fault you for that."

Horton gave him a troubled look. "You...aren't planning anything, are you?"

K'nidMin glanced at the overcast sky and gave her a solemn ear twitch. "There's a major storm coming in. I can assure you our contact herd would be *er'trxxda* to go out in weather like that."

Horton gave him a skeptical look. "I...suppose."

"And I *suppose* your people wouldn't be thrilled about going out there in a major storm either?"

"Well, no, we wouldn't."

They were interrupted by a brief sprinkle and a chill breeze, causing Horton to shiver. "Not to mention the Flyers have rarely been seen out in major weather," K'nidMin added. "So it's unlikely we could meet them anyway."

"There is that." Horton's aura showed she suspected something.

"And I like to think I care about my people, as do you."

"I'm...certain you do."

"So it seems you won't have anything to report to your superiors after all, does it?" The wind picked up a bit more, chilling them. "In fact, our herd could use a bit of rest, so this storm comes at an opportune moment." K'nidMin glanced at R'nemReth, then took her hand in his. "As for us, we thought we would take a little *private* time and get to know each other better." He offered a cynical smile. "Like you humans say, all work and no play..."

Horton studied them both for a long moment. "Well," she said at last. "Good luck...on getting to know each other."

§

"All work and no play, hmmm?" R'nemReth grumbled as they headed for the quarters building. "You have a real talent for lying. At least I *hope* you were lying."

K'nidMin chuckled. "You learn a lot of interesting skills on field assignments. And you might save your hopes for more urgent matters."

She ignored the double implication. "Will she report us?"

K'nidMin glanced at her. "She's on our side. As long as we give her some cover, she'll cover us in turn. She wants the herd to succeed as much as we do. Not all humans are *un'tdars*."

§

They spent the evening preparing for their trip, which meant packing rations, first aid kits and climbing gear into straddle packs. In addition to the pack, each of them had a coil of rope and a portable shelter. Along with the gray utilities and heavy duty footsocks they issued her, she also had a waterproof overtunic. She paused as she was about to pack it and pondered its dull mottled browns and greens. "Are you sure it's wise to wear camouflage when we want them to see us?"

K'nidMin faltered, and his aura was tinted with embarrassment. "Good point," he muttered. "I'll give you credit: you're at the gallop on this."

She couldn't help but notice his warming sense of respect for her. "So what do we do?" she asked. "I don't want to get rained on. We could get sick, which would sincerely knot our tails on this Fuster Cluck."

K'nidMin pondered for a bit then stepped to the window to study the sky, which looked ominous. "We'll need them if the forecast is correct. We'll take them along, but only wear them if it rains."

She went back to sorting through her gear, trying to decide what to leave and what to stuff into her straddle pack. Zero-G rations, as much as she loathed them, were obvious. She sorted out the worst of them, and packed some protean bars to substitute. An extra set of footsocks...a first aid kit...

"Do we really need this climbing gear?" She waved at a pile of improvised metal pins, snap rings and a small hammer—heavy and unpleasant to think about. "I thought we weren't going into the mountains?"

K'nidMin paused and surveyed her pack. "We won't go high up, but even the foothills will have their rough spots."

"I don't know how to climb mountains!"

"It's just a safety precaution. Trust me: if either of us is injured, we'll be a long way from help. We'll rig safety lines wherever we find a hazardous patch." He offered her a reassuring ear twitch. "I know its a burden, but better safe than sorry."

She hefted her pack, dismayed by its weight. "Do we need all this stuff? This *l'cc'vn* thing weighs."

K'nidMin offered an amused ear twitch. "Don't complain. A standard 'Dark Grays' combat pack weighs three times as much, plus weaponry."

She looked askance at him. "It does, eh? Remind me never to join the 'Dark Grays'!"

"Remember: never join the 'Dark Grays'."

"Um...right."

She went back to packing, and after thinking about it, included the metal gear. As she worked, she kept sneaking occasional glances at him. She could tell he cared about her. She wasn't used to that and it felt good, even if there was an implied 'personal interest' attached to it.

About that: he was fairly handsome, and had a quick, wry sense of humor which she felt was one of his more redeeming features. And there was an aura about him, an aura of self reliance, of decisive action which matched her temperament well. She pondered him as she sorted and stuffed. As far as she could see he was not a wise choice. No doubt he would be gone on his assignments perhaps for years at a time, and there was the constant risk of his being killed. Then there was the prospect of having to pack up everything and follow him to some Ancestor-forsaken frontier world. She heard stories of the dangers of getting involved with a Service member. No, as likable as he was, he was not a wise choice at all.

But then...he was smart and capable, a good leader, not afraid to make the tough decisions...a galloper in the 'Dark Grays'. He cared about her, admired her. She recalled that ear nibble earlier; the memory of his open sign of affection warmed her. And he wasn't bad looking.

'You're being foolish!' she thought to herself. She couldn't be sure they'd be alive tomorrow, and even if they succeeded, there were no end of very real barriers in her path. She sighed, and hurried with her packing.

It was late when they finished, and both were exhausted. "We need to get some sleep," K'nidMin said. "I hope to make an early start tomorrow." A gust of rain pattered on the roof. "Our luck, it'll be pouring."

§

Sure enough, by early next morning it was raining lightly, so after a quick first-meal of protean bars they struggled into their overtunics and headed out. There were only a few watch-standers stirring at this hour, and K'nidMin used their overtunics to hide their straddle packs from the humans as they crossed the compound. Arbiter G'nemBrik and K'nidMin's Worthy were waiting when they arrived at the Arbiter's grotto.

"Are you sure you want to do this?" G'nemBrik asked. "The latest report is this storm has shifted west. We're looking for at least a full day of rain, perhaps two."

"There's nothing for it, sir," K'nidMin said. "If we don't succeed, we might as well pack up and go home." He then turned to his Worthy. "You'll need to stall for the next couple of days. Keep everyone busy so the humans won't notice we're gone."

"Suppose they start asking?"

K'nidMin glanced at R'nemReth. "I already mentioned to Horton that we plan to spend some *private* time together. Perhaps a few off-color remarks dropped *casually* will give them a reason for our absence."

His Worthy chuckled. "You are shameless. The humans will lap it up."

The morning was getting on, and people were stirring. A brief gust of wind heralded more rain, causing them to pull their overtunics tighter. "I can only hope you know what you're doing," G'nemBrik said, mournfully. "May your Ancestors watch over you both."

§

She gave him a surly look as they headed for one of the side gates manned by their people. "Are you this *M'mendoch* on all your missions? I thought you 'Dark Grays' were oh-so tail-knotted about discipline and procedure."

"One of the nice things about an independent specialist herd is one can operate...shall we say, 'informally'."

"Informally? It must be wonderful to go your whole career in an out-of-control stampede!"

He laughed out loud. "It has its moments."

She didn't share his sense of humor under the circumstances. "Have you ever faced a tail-knot like this before?"

He offered an awkward ear twitch. "Actually...this is our second contact mission. The first was with the Li-qua, and they were handed to us all wrapped up in pretty paper." Her dismayed look brought on further explanations. "They were contacted by your brother when he was stranded on their world. By time we were called in, they had been relocated to Checkpoint and the Learnéds were already there in force. It was pretty much a training exercise."

That shook her. "So you have no idea what you're doing?"

He offered a sardonic ear twitch. "No, but we *are* the experts, after all."

*****

121

"A Desperate Move"

They set out during a rain squall which they hoped would hide their movement from the human sentries. It must have worked: no one came after them. The watch humans must have figured no one would be so *er'trxxda* as to head into Flyer country alone in this weather, if they were even noticed at all...or perhaps it was Lieutenant Horton running 'interference' again. Either way, their departure went unremarked.

Just to be sure, they headed up the coast until the base was lost in the distance, then circled wide and headed into the foothills. Their path took them well away from the river and into the area where the native herd beasts grazed. They were able to steer past the herds, who moved reluctantly to avoid them anyway, but they couldn't help being aware of them. The herds avoided them, but their stench remained so it wasn't long before both were gasping in the foul air. R'nemReth plodded along wearily, dodging mounds of herd beast droppings and grumbling to herself all the while. Her footsocks were soaked (she didn't like to think with what), her *l'cc'vn* straddle pack was digging into her back, and she was overheating from the damp chill. This wasn't the first time she'd been caught in the rain, but familiarity didn't make it any easier.

At one point they came upon some freshly disturbed earth plowed up by several massive grooves. "Flyers," K'nidMin said as he examined them. "This is where one of them scored a kill." He paced off the gouges and his aura was not happy. "These are claw marks."

"Those are some *p'quas'tka* big claws." R'nemReth was dismayed at their size. "They could easily carry us off."

K'nidMin gave her a reassuring smile, not that his aura shared his optimism. "Don't worry. We'll make contact and everything will work out. You'll see."

"I *hope* so." She was shaken by the size and power of the creature who made those gouges and carried a herd beast away, alive and kicking, to be eaten. Seeing them from a distance was one thing, looking down at their claw marks was something else entirely. "I have a bad feeling about this."

"Be brave, R'nemReth. If you stay calm when we meet them, your telepathy will get us through."

'If I can stay calm,' she thought to herself.

K'nidMin moved on. She struggled with her straddle pack to ease the strain in her back, and trudged after him.

§

The rain seemed to go on forever, a steady, depressing drizzle which made the footing treacherous. The day grew late as they trudged along. The ground changed from flat grassland to low, rolling country as they approached the foothills. She slipped more than once on the greasy undergrowth, and paused more than once to dig stickly bush thorns out of her legs, but was too weary by then to curse her ill-fortune. K'nidMin went on ahead, making better time than she could so she had to struggle to keep up. She silently cursed him for not recognizing that she wasn't as fit as him, and didn't have his tough service physique to keep her going.

"How long do we keep this up?" she asked after a while.

K'nidMin paused and looked back at her. "Tired?"

"And sore, and hungry, and dripping wet," she complained.

"Sorry." His aura was a mix of embarrassment and gnawing worry, and as he glanced around the sky she realized he was anxious to reach the forest cover of the foothills.

"It's alright," she said as she caught up with him. "But I really need to take a break."

"Yes. Me too." K'nidMin scanned the area ahead: they were nearing the first outcrop of trees on the edge of the foothills. "The rain is thinning. We'll see what shelter we can find under the forest, then we'll stop for a meal."

§

They found a spot of high ground sheltered by the forest canopy and out of the steady breeze. R'nemReth shucked her straddle pack and sagged in the driest spot she could find with a weary sigh. "I let you talk me into this," she grumbled.

K'nidMin offered a sympathetic ear twitch. "I know it's not easy, but it needs to be done and you have good reasons for doing it." He gave her a reassuring smile. "You're doing fine. Long marches are always tiring."

He dug into his straddle pack and came up with a small portable *V'liz* cooker powered by a canned flame. For a wonder, he soon had steaming bowls ready. "Here. A hot drink will make you feel better." She accepted it gratefully, luxuriating in the warmth and the physical boost it gave. "Soak your Number Five ration in it," he suggested. "It'll taste better."

It did. A full belly and a bowl of hot *V'liz* made her feel somewhat alive again. "How far have we come?" she asked as she looked around at the dismal landscape. It all looked the same shrouded in patchy mists, and she wouldn't have recognized landmarks anyway.

K'nidMin dug out a small inertial tracker and studied it. "We're at the end of the valley. These woods are at the start of the foothills. We've made good time." He tucked the tracker away and studied her. "You did good for someone not used to this."

"Whatever. I've had enough for one day. I say we set up camp and get some rest before tackling those hills."

K'nidMin didn't seem thrilled. "The day is still young. We can make a lot more progress before dark."

"I'm worn out!" she snapped at him. "My feet ache, and I'm cold and wet, and I'm not going any further! You don't seem to care that I'm not cut out for this!"

He hesitated for a long moment, with a mournful aura. "You're right," he said at last. "I didn't stop to think. I'm sorry."

It wasn't often she received an apology from someone, and it dampened her angst a bit. "The day's almost over anyway," she mumbled.

He pondered her silently, and she could sense his mood changing. "I guess I'm a bit nervous about all this," he said at last. "It's one thing to risk myself, but I feel guilty risking you, too."

She offered a weary ear twitch as her mood settled. "Thank you. I shouldn't have snapped at you."

"No harm done. Let's get settled in, shall we?" The air was cleared between them, and they set to for the evening.

Setting up camp wasn't as simple as it sounded, made worse by physical exhaustion. It took her forever to get her personal shelter put up; K'nidMin had his done and came to help her before she could make sense of it. Once it was ready, she crawled into it with a grateful sigh, and pulled off her sopping footsocks. K'nidMin kept busy erecting a small fly between their shelters to protect their gear and to park his *V'liz* cooker under.

"A few hours rest and you'll feel better," he said. "Tomorrow will be a bit easier; you'll be getting used to it by then."

"I don't *want* to get used to it," she grumbled.

K'nidMin settled into his own shelter facing her. "I know this is difficult," he said, earnestly. "Life out here on the frontier is often hard. You can do it, and it's for a good cause." He offered an encouraging ear-twitch. "Have faith in yourself. I do."

"Thank you," she mumbled. "I'm sorry to be such a fuss. I'm just tired, is all."

"It's more than that," he said, gently. "You're still feeling down about your situation." He was watching her earnestly in the fading light, reading her emotions with his enhanced empathy. "Don't be so hard on yourself. You're stronger than you realize; I can see it in you." His aura was warm and supportive. "You'll come through."

Now that she had some time, she found herself in an introspective mood, and reflected on where she was and how she got here. She was still surprised by how her life changed since that day in the Peace Warden lockup, and that she was on a distant world deep in human space searching for a race of dangerous aliens. The whole concept bemused her. But then, as strange and difficult as this was, it was a solid break with her past. She used to dream of adventures; now she was living one. She reflected on all the interesting characters who came into her life: Loo-loo-ba, Horton, Sergeant MacIntosh, J J Ballas, K'nidMin. Especially K'nidMin. As difficult as her present situation was, she was thankful to have met so many fine, *interesting* people. Now that she thought about it, she couldn't imagine ever returning to the street after knowing them.

Come to which, her curiosity was stirred by thinking of K'nidMin. "Why do you do this?" she asked. "Being in the Service must be tough enough, not to mention galloping around some Ancestorless places like this."

He sighed. "It's my own fault, I guess. I've never been one to sit still. This is rough and dangerous duty, and there are times when I'm genuinely afraid, but I just can't face the idea of doing something ordinary for the rest of my life. The idea of being on the staff..." His aura took a chill, and he offered a sardonic ear twitch. "I'd make a very poor bureaucrat."

She offered a derisive snort. "I can't see you shuffling paper all day."

"Thank you!" He grinned at her. "No, this is what I was destined for. Think of it: we're out here on the cutting edge, beyond the borders of our known Universe. Who knows what we might find around the next bend?"

She understood what he was saying, and she felt his excitement. "You need to go around that next bend, don't you?"

He nodded. "And to the next star system, the next galaxy. I love the thought of meeting new alien races. That's why I like the humans so much, as obnoxious as they can be at times."

She recognized in his words her lonely daydreams from when she was an outcast on the street. It put a new perspective on him, which she liked. "I envy you."

"I'm not exactly the enviable sort, I guess. I suppose I'm pretty ragged at times."

"Better that than some spit-and-polish *un'tdar* like the Fleet First!"

He pondered for a bit. "There's some real antagonism between you two, isn't there?" he said, gently.

"It's not my fault!" Her frustrations came welling up out of her. "I was a victim! I never asked to be cursed with these *ui'DmukNa* psychic powers!"

"I know."

"My mother, C'traBenla, she accepted me for who I am. Why can't he? I'm his hatchling too!"

"I don't pretend to understand these things," he said softly. "I can only guess the Ki-Elder is invested in you, like the humans invest in their offspring. They put a lot of emotion into their young. Maybe he feels you aren't living up to his vision of his descendants."

"You mean like Captain Pencroft, son and grandson of somebody? If that's what the Ki-Elder hopes for, it doesn't speak much for his character!"

K'nidMin offered a rueful ear twitch. "Point taken. Still, the principle applies even when there are exceptions. It's in our nature to view our surroundings as what is right and normal. His problem is you don't fit into his preconceived world."

She brooded for a time as the twilight deepened. "I wish I could fit in, or at least that he'd accept me for who I am."

"Honestly, I don't think you would do well in his world. You're too independent."

She recognized the truth in that, which was a minor revelation. "Still, I'd feel better if he wasn't so bitter toward me."

"You'll earn his respect; trust me."

The gentle rushing of the stream and the sounds of small animals filled the brooding silence. She sagged in her shelter and scanned the woods around them, dim in the fading light. "Are there any dangerous animals out here?"

She could sense K'nidMin's concern. "I don't know. Aside from the herd beasts, the only life forms we've been able to study were small creatures found around the encampment." He dug around in his shelter and came up with a sidearm. "Hopefully we won't need anything bigger than this."

"Wonderful! You came out here not knowing what we might run into?"

"It can take centuries to really understand a planet's ecosystem. We're still finding new life forms in remote corners of d'enchia. We've only been here a short time, and we have more urgent priorities."

The wind picked up, sending a flush of heat through her. "I give up!" She tugged her overtunic tighter. "I'm cold! How am I going to get to sleep when I'm hyper from the chill?"

K'nidMin's aura grew concerned. "You do need to sleep. I have something which will help." He struggled out of his shelter, dug through his straddle pack, and came up with a folded piece of something shiny. "Here. Wrap yourself in this thermal blanket. It traps your body heat, which will slow your metabolism."

The blanket proved to be a large sheet of tough plastic with a thin metallic coating on one side. She struggled with it in the confines of her shelter, and managed to wrap it around her. In no time she was turning drowsy as her metabolism slowed.

"*Ancestors*, that feels good!" she sighed. "Thank you, K'nidMin."

"Get some sleep." His words were tinted by the unspoken warmth of his aura. Her last thought as she drifted off was how nice it felt to have K'nidMin thinking of her.

§

The next morning was cold and damp, although the rain had dwindled to a chill drizzle. R'nemReth lay curled up in her thermal blanket, aching from yesterday's trek and a night sleeping on the ground. At least she was warm.

"Good morning." K'nidMin intruded on her drowsy state by waving a steaming bowl in front of her. "How do you feel this morning?"

"I try not to." She struggled to free one arm from the blanket and took the bowl. It contained something thick and chunky, fragrant of *V'liz*. "*V'liz* stew?" She sampled it cautiously.

"The Number Five ration makes a decent stew when you dice up the contents." K'nidMin said. It did. The *V'liz* masked the worst of the ration's taste, and the warmth was welcome. "There's more if you want."

Despite how she felt, she was grateful to him for thinking of her with the tarp, and now the hot bowl. "So what's the plan for today?"

K'nidMin pondered the landscape around them, his mind filled with doubt. "It'll be rougher going from here on. We're into the foothills now, and we should set a slower pace so you won't be so tired."

She thought on it for a bit as she savored the last of her stew. "How far will we go? Do you expect to climb those mountains to get to them?"

"No. We'll go as far as we reasonably can while our rations last. That should take us fairly high up, but not into the mountains. If they don't spot us by then, we'll give up and turn back."

She pondered the journey ahead wearily, and something in her spirit changed almost without her realizing it. "We should go as far as we have to. We can stretch our rations if need be."

K'nidMin pondered her for a time. "You're desperate to get that Writ, aren't you?"

"It's more than just the Writ. My own father was ready to let me rot in a penal nest rather than have me around as an embarrassment. I intend to rub his snout in this so he'll know he was wrong about me."

K'nidMin nodded solemnly. "You've reached the turning point; good." There was something in his aura which said she'd passed some sort of test.

"A turning point?"

"All recruits go through this. Being in the 'Dark Grays' isn't easy. It takes a special dedication, a special kind of courage, to carry the load. You're at the point where hardship has become a challenge, not a burden."

She felt a special sense of accomplishment in his words. "Will it be easier from here on?"

"No, but you've taken its measure. You're one of us now."

She could tell 'us' meant more than just wearing a gray uniform. She had more than passed a test: she had changed from a loser on the street into something better. She basked in his aura of admiration and respect, and swore to herself the Ki-Elder would eat his words.

"We'll need to get out of these woods if we expect them to spot us." As much as she appreciated K'nidMin's desire to reach the safety of the forest, that was no longer needed.

K'nidMin studied the landscape ahead. "You're right. We need to aim for that ridge line." He gestured to a rolling ridge of bare ground faintly visible through the trees to their right. "It'll be easier going over open ground."

§

It took rest of the day and another meal break before they reached the high ground. By that time they were well up into the foothills. Even in the open the going was slow and treacherous, their way often blocked by rock outcroppings or small, fast streams which tumbled down the ridge to the river winding its way from the mountains to the coast.

"Ancestors, this water is cold!" she grumbled as they forded yet another stream. The current and the slippery rocks threatened to sweep her off her feet, and she had to struggle to make any headway.

K'nidMin was on the far bank taking up a line tied around her shoulders and looped around a convenient tree. Although the stream was narrow it was swollen by the rain, making these crossings treacherous. "Don't complain," he called to her, and gestured to the main river below them. "That river is glacial runoff, far worse."

The steady rush of the stream masked her grumbling. By time she scrambled up on the far bank she was jittery from the cold. K'nidMin wrapped her thermal blanket around her. "Let's take a break." They settled on the bank, too weary to go any further.

"How much more will we do today?" she asked as she nibbled a protean bar.

K'nidMin pondered the overcast sky. "It's getting late, and we're both tired. This is a good spot to camp."

She was too weary and wet to argue. They turned to, and she had her shelter set up in short order while K'nidMin fired up his *V'liz* heater. By the time he offered her a steaming bowl, she was wrapped in her thermal blanket, as comfortable as could be for the moment.

"You catch on fast." His aura was warm with approval.

"You might say I was motivated." She followed his advice of crumbling her Number Five ration into the bowl, and attacked it greedily. She was hungry enough so the taste was bearable. "I thought you said open ground would be easier."

He offered a rueful ear twitch. "I didn't design this world."

"Well when you do design one, be sure to include public transportation."

Something caught K'nidMin's eye. "Flyers." He pointed off to their left, across the river. A hand or more of them were faintly visible in the distant mists, sweeping down a ridge line in a broad rank.

"They don't look like another hunting party. I wonder what they're up to?"

"They're searching for us. We must have been spotted earlier." He nodded grimly as they watched the flight fade into the distance. "They lost us in the forest, so they're conducting search sweeps."

"Will they find us?"

"It's only a matter of time if they keep at it." He scanned the sky in all directions, but there was no sign of a second search. "We're probably alright for the moment, but we'll likely be spotted tomorrow."

"This is *er'trxxda*," she grumbled. "We're stirring up no end of fuss! They won't be in a friendly mood when they find us."

K'nidMin paused and looked at her. "I'm counting on them knowing the risk we're taking," he said, somberly. "My hope is the Flyers will realize this suicidal move means we seriously want to reach them."

"I hope you're right." As frightening as the thought of death was, her strongest emotion was frustration. Being killed meant failure, and she was grimly determined to rub the Fleet First's snout in her success.

He turned away and pondered the landscape ahead of them. "We don't have any guarantees, but the risk is worth it. At least we're getting a reaction from them."

*****

"Contact!"

The weather cleared by the next morning, and they found themselves under unusually bright, open skies, for this world. "This will make it easy for them to spot us," K'nidMin muttered as he scanned the horizon in all directions.

"Well that's what we want, isn't it?"

He gave her a somber look. "Yes, but hopefully we can meet under favorable circumstances. It wouldn't do for them to just swoop down and capture us."

The thought chilled her. "Hopefully."

That reminded them of how vulnerable their location was, so it took them only moments to break camp and continue their journey. They were well up into the foothills by then. Before long, their ridge line blended into the shallow lower slopes of the first mountains. Continuing along the slope was difficult, awkward walking. The temperature rose, so they were actually feeling sluggish by mid-morning. The occasional fording of chilly streams was a welcome change. The ground rose slowly but steadily, with occasional tumbled rock outcroppings, so they had to pause several times to find places to scramble over the obstructions. That ate up both time and energy, and they stopped at mid-day to catch their breath after one such climb.

"I had to be ambitious," she grumbled as she worked through a Number Four endurance ration. "This is my own *l'cc'vn* fault for wanting to knot the Ki-Elder's tail."

"That seems like a noble purpose," K'nidMin said with a wry grin. "You have something to live for now."

"I suppose." She finished her ration and sagged wearily on the damp undergrowth. She was feeling a lot less eager than she did last evening, and was worried about their inevitable meeting with the Flyers. She could well imagine how they would react to their territory being invaded; all of a sudden she was afraid. "I have a bad feeling about this. We may be taking one gamble too many."

He gave her a considered ear twitch and his aura was full of concern. "It's more of a calculated risk."

"But still it's a risk."

He pondered her for a moment. "You were all first-finger about this yesterday," he said, gently. "I can understand if you're losing your nerve."

"I guess maybe I am, a little. I keep thinking about what could happen if this doesn't work."

He nodded. "Sometimes, if you want to get ahead in life, you have to take chances," he said, earnestly. "Your being here shows you understand that."

"All it shows is how desperate I was at the time! And what's so 'calculated' about this, anyway?"

"The 'calculated' part is your telepathic ability. That stacks the game in our favor. You watch: we'll get the treaty."

She wasn't entirely convinced of that, or of her abilities, and it left her feeling kind of hollow. "Still...we're putting our lives on the line here. We've done everything we could reasonably be expected to do. They can't ask you to be killed for a treaty."

"Actually, they can," he said, somberly. "This is what the 'Dark Grays'—any military service—is about. We take the chances ordinary people aren't equipped to take, nor should they be." He studied her for a long moment, no doubt sensing her unease and uncertainty. "Sometimes our people must gamble in order to achieve some desirable goal. We 'Dark Grays' are the wager."

She already knew that, but the idea stuck in her throat. "They can't expect you to die for a piece of paper. It's not like the Flyers are a threat like the humans. We don't *have* to win this one."

He gave her a vexed ear twitch. "It's not just about us, or the Flyers. We can't allow the Joint First Contact program to fail. It's too new and untried, and it will be vital in the future. That's the prize we're gambling for."

She was sensitive to his anxious mood, and wondered why he was so defensive. "Will you be in trouble if you can't deliver? Will they demote you or put you in some *x'mnnb'* assignment?"

He answered with a rude noise. "Hardly! The worst would be that I go back in the line pool; I'd wind up in command of an echelon of the fleet defender herd, which would be easy compared to this. But everything we worked so long for would collapse. We can't allow that to happen."

She pondered that as the silence stretched out. If it wasn't personal fear, his motivation must be something deeper. "Are you afraid to fail, K'nidMin?" she asked, gently.

He was a long time answering. "I guess I am," he said at last. "I hate admitting defeat."

That brought back a memory of something her mother said:

'That would be admitting defeat, and you hate to admit defeat.'

It seemed *s'vem'grott* was a trait of a good Elder, and as much as she loathed the Fleet First, she was favorably impressed with K'nidMin's determination. But then, this didn't seem like a good moment to be *s'vem'grott*. "You should get a pass on this one. The humans tail-knotted this deal, so why risk our lives for something which is their fault?"

"Fault has nothing to do with it." He stared off into the distance for a bit, his mind in turmoil. "This mission is important, vital. We *have* to succeed despite the humans, which means we *have* to take risks."

That dismayed her. He was determined to go on despite the danger to his own life, and more importantly hers, when he had a perfect excuse to accept failure and walk away. "Why? Is it worth getting killed for your precious career?"

"It's not about me, and it's not about the Flyers," he said, sternly. "And it's certainly not just about my career." He brooded in silence for some time, his aura churning with mixed emotions. "There's more at stake here. Relations with the humans have been deteriorating for years. We nearly went to war with them not long ago, and from what I hear, the political trends on earth are ominous." He turned and looked at her. "Anything which gets us and the humans working together for the common good can make a difference in the future. The success of this joint mission will reach beyond the here and now."

She was bewildered by that. "You don't really think you can change the course of history, do you?"

"Perhaps not. But each of us has to try, to do what we can. We can't just leave peace to chance."

As foreign as that was to her experience, she couldn't find fault with his argument. Self-sacrifice for the common good was an alien concept in her young life, but there was no way of avoiding the truth of it; especially out here. The thought of risking her life...of perhaps dying...for the society which turned against her was hard to accept. She understood K'nidMin's choice and respected him for it, however reluctantly, but for her...

...for her there was another reason, which she was only beginning to understand. If she was ever to be free, if she ever wanted to be accepted into the Ic'nichi people, she needed to rise above the street. This self-sacrifice was one of the harsh lessons she needed to learn if she ever wanted to be more than one of the 'lost younglings'. All she had to look forward to back on d'enchia was life in a penal nest. She had to 'walk through the valley of the shadow of death', as K'nidMin put it. Her road to the future lay over these hills. She sighed, hefted her straddle pack, and trudged after him.

§

A short time later, K'nidMin paused to rear up and look off to their left. "Flyers." He pointed out another search sweep working along the nearer bank of the main river.

"Persistent, aren't they?" she muttered.

"They seem to be taking our intrusion seriously. All this search effort must be taxing their resources."

"What resources?"

He paused and turned to look at her. "Labor: primitive societies don't have our labor-saving technology. Each Flyer can only do one thing at a time, and their ordinary lives must take up a large part of their day. All this effort must be a huge strain on their economy."

That was something she never thought of before, and it put the Flyers in a new perspective. She could well imagine how their lives were being disrupted by this intrusion. "They won't be happy with us, will they?"

"Perhaps not." K'nidMin watched while the Flyer sweep faded into the distance. His aura was not pleased.

"How much farther are we going to go?"

135

He studied the landscape around them, which wasn't promising. They were on the lower slope of an outlying mountain, a steep grade of loose broken stones and dirt with no cover in sight. Ahead lay a twisted slope thrusting deep into the mountains. To their right, some distance further up-slope, was a sheer rock face. To their left, the slope tumbled down to the banks of the major river with a narrow path along its edge. The Flyers assumed, reasonably, they went that way, but it wouldn't be long before they broadened their search pattern. There was no cover on the slope other than underbrush and the occasional scraggly tree.

"We need to find cover," K'nidMin said. "They will find us shortly, so our goal is the nearest stand of trees."

§

Easier said than done. This world, for all its rain, was not particularly forested, and the trees there were scraggly things to begin with. Their worry turned more and more to frustration as they struggled along over the rough slope. It wasn't long before R'nemReth was so weary that she was starting to lose her footing. Even their constant fear and grim determination didn't compensate for aching muscles and much-abused feet.

Finally, after her fourth or fifth tumble, it was just too much. She shrugged off her straddle pack and broke down crying bitterly. K'nidMin slogged his way back to her and tried to comfort her. "Are you alright?"

She nodded, and tried to choke back her tears. "I...I'm just tired, is all."

"I know." He scanned the horizon nervously, then dug some protean bars out of his pack and offered her one. "We can take a brief break."

She lay on her side for some time, nibbling the protean bar and wishing for a bowl of *V'liz*. Like every good thing in her life, she could only wish. "This will go on forever, won't it?"

He offered an encouraging ear twitch. "We'll find a spot soon. You're doing great; this is a tough march for any new tail."

She was silent for a bit, wondering about the future, or if they even had a future. "I feel lost. It's like we're trapped in the Uttermost Darkness. I don't know what to do any more."

136

His aura was tinted with concern. "We're not lost. We're way out beyond the edges of our known Universe, but we're not lost: believe in that." His words rang with firm belief, as did his aura. She was able to take some small comfort from his certainty.

"This is your world, isn't it? Out here beyond the beyond?"

"Yes, as a matter of fact." He offered a smile. "It has its moments, like now. But then I'd rather be here than stuck in a cubby hole in the Staff. You talk about being lost: *that* is being lost. I pity those poor *hro'n'nad n'bna'nmn*. They don't even have the courage to resign and get a real job out in the world." He shook his head in dismay. "Those sorry *P'grrt'ps* are truly lost!"

She could understand his feelings; what he described was way too much like life on the street. She gave him a somber look. "We could die out here, today." In an odd way, the thought didn't terrify her so much as it did earlier.

"Yes, we could. But at least we will have lived."

She pondered that for a bit, and decided he was right. "What are our chances?"

"That depends on you," he said, evenly. "You're our wedge; you have the power to make this happen. Can you hold together when the moment comes?"

She wasn't entirely sure, but her grim determination to try was coming back. "I'll hold together."

"Then I'd say our odds are good." He finished his protean bar, struggled to his feet, and scanned the horizon again. "We better get moving. We don't want to be caught in the open, and if we squat here any longer we'll start to freeze up."

She struggled to her feet and stretched to get the stiffness out of her back. "If we pull this off, you'll be able to get more resources for your herd, won't you?"

"No doubt."

She stretched her neck to try and relieve her stiffness. "Then see if you can get a physical therapist assigned to the herd. A thorough massage would be a gift from the Ancestors right now."

He chuckled. "That's what I like about you: always thinking of yourself."

§

Mid-day faded into afternoon as they slogged along. Both had their second wind by then, but the going was tough as the cross-grade grew steeper. They slipped repeatedly, setting off mini-avalanches of gravel and loose stones. It seemed for every step forward they took another sideways, and before long the unnatural gait had them both aching.

"This is hopeless!" she grumbled. "Can't we move further down slope to where the footing is better?"

He studied the landscape ahead. "It won't help. See those rocks down there?" He gestured to a field of jumbled boulders along the main river. "That will be tough going, and there isn't any cover down there." He came back to where she was and took her hand. "I know this is rough, but we don't have much farther to go. We'll find a patch of woods and make our stand soon."

§

They plowed on, weariness, desperation, and dogged endurance struggling for control. They were aching, footsore, overheated and numb with fatigue; focussing on the sloped gravel ahead as if nothing else existed.

Some time later K'nidMin staggered to a halt and looked off to their left. "There's another flight." He pointed out a group of five sweeping along the lower slopes across the river not more than two thousand lengths away.

"Will they see us?"

K'nidMin watched as the flight swept on ahead of them. "They're focussed on the ground. They missed us this time, but it looks like they're expanding the search." Both of them were *r'vebbe* by the near miss, and by the sure knowledge they would be spotted on the next sweep. He turned to her once they were gone. "Last chance: we might be able to hide in those rocks if we move fast, and retreat after dark. You sure you want to go on?"

She hardly needed her empathic powers to know he was afraid, enough so that he was ready to abandon principle and look to their safety. She was afraid too. This was no longer a theory or a wishful plan: their being discovered was only a matter of time, not very much time, and the Flyers would be in a bad mood. But as he said earlier that morning, this was about more than just them.

"We came here for a reason," she said, nervously. "It's too late for regrets now."

"You embarrass me," he muttered with a shaky ear twitch. He took one last searching look around, then without another word he turned and trotted on ahead.

Privately she was glad he didn't argue since she was about ready to stampede in any random direction. Instead she struggled to adjust her straddle pack, which was digging into her spine, and followed as fast as she could. They headed further along the slope, keeping an anxious lookout in all directions. As much as they tried to keep a steady pace, it wasn't long before they were in a nervous trot, then in what passed for a full gallop in the treacherous footing. Soon they were panting and gasping for breath as they fought their way along the slope.

It seemed to go on forever as they scrambled over the unstable ground, kicking up endless small rock slides. Her feet were in agony from stepping on loose stones, but she ignored the pain as she struggled to keep up. With their forced bravado stripped away, they both succumbed to fear, running for their lives in search of some shelter anywhere ahead. All thoughts of meeting the Flyers were forgotten in their mad stampede. They were both exhausted, running on sheer panic, but their advance was nightmarishly slow and those trees might have been on d'enchia for all their efforts.

Just when it seemed they couldn't go another step, a clump of scraggly forest appeared around the shoulder of the mountain ahead. "Head for those trees!" K'nidMin called to her as he waved vaguely at the woods ahead. "We can meet...on even terms."

The sight thrilled her, giving her a brief, badly needed burst of energy. They would be safe from the Flyers in those woods, and would be able to negotiate once they were discovered. In any case they were both too winded to run much further. She galloped as fast as she could, an unsteady, shambling trot over the loose footing, driven by fear and weighed down by her heavy pack. They were in very real danger unless they could gain time to connect with the Flyers who found them. Her long worries about what could happen at this moment were all too vivid, giving her the extra energy she needed for this final dash.

They were caught by surprise as another flight of four appeared over the patch of woods ahead of them, strung out in a search line which actually overflew them before they broke formation with a shrill cry and circled back at them.

K'nidMin shook off his surprise and turned to her urgently. "Reach out to them! Quickly!"

The flight were coming at them fast, flapping their wings at a furious pace. She shook off her panic and reached out to them. *'We come in peace! We are trying to end this conflict! Please talk to us!'*

They didn't respond. Instead they spread out, the first two circling wide around their flanks while the last two came straight on. "That's their hunting pattern!" K'nidMin said. "I don't like the look of this."

He was right: the two flankers were herding them together, keeping them from stampeding, just like they did with the herd beasts. She threw a quick nervous glance at the woods a mere hundred lengths away, if that. It was too far; they'd never make it. She fought down her panic by sheer strength and tried desperately to connect with them. *'We are your friends! We came to talk with your leaders!'*

K'nidMin finally yielded to panic and turned to her. "They're attacking! Run!" A moment later, as he turned for the woods, the first Flyer swooped and grabbed him, carrying him aloft effortlessly.

She lost it and ran in panic, crashing headlong into brush and saplings as she fled for the shelter of the woods. She didn't get far: a vast shadow passed overhead, a set of enormous claws grabbed her around her middle with crushing force, and the next thing she knew she was being carried aloft.

*****

"War Or Peace?"

She was pretty well cried out and sunk into fatal despair by time they reached the Flyer's lair in the depths of the mountains. The journey was a nightmare hallucination of vertigo and terror, and what rational thought she could muster was spent obsessing over whether she would be killed and eaten or eaten alive.

She hardly noticed or cared as the flight circled a steep valley high amid the mountain peaks, then descended toward a broad plateau. The valley opened out around them, the mountain sides dotted with large nests of woven branches amid the rocks and scraggly trees. A stream came tumbling down from snowy heights, coursing through scattered woods, and vanished into the distant foothills.

As they descended, they were met by a swarm of Flyers who greeted their captors with loud, shrill cries. Before she realized, they were descending over the plateau, and the Flyer carrying her released her. She landed in a heap with a cry of pain, and curled up into a ball to await the end. Then K'nidMin was there, limping from a scraped left leg. "Are you alright?" Her angst and terror overwhelmed her, and she broke down shaking and sobbing. "You need to pull yourself together!"

They were surrounded by Flyers perched on every open spot along the edge of the plateau. They were enormous, fully grown adults with endless teeth and claws. The plateau was littered with bones and scraps of hide. She recoiled when she realized this was their feeding ground. "They're going to eat us!" she whimpered.

He dragged her forcefully to her feet. "We're still alive! They must want something! This is our chance to communicate with them. We're committed, so you need to calm down and focus!"

One thing she'd learned on the street was to keep cool in a crisis. It took strength she never imagined having, but she was able to pull herself together. "I...I'll be...alright," she mumbled as she fought back her tears.

K'nidMin gave her a searching look, and through her panic she could sense his concern for her. "Good! We need to know the equation; what does your empathy tell us?"

141

She fought with her emotions, forcing her terror down by main strength, and looked around them. The plateau was filled with Flyers, with more arriving by the moment. A large one squatted on a bit of rock with a second laying at her feet. The rest gathered around them in a broad ring, arguing among themselves in a thunderous volley of high-pitched cries.

"That one," she gestured at the one on the rock. "That's their leader." She focussed her telepathic power on her. *'She is called the White-Wing,'* she added telepathically since the noise was so great they could hardly hear each other.

'What about the one laying down?'

She focussed again. *'He is the Gray-Wing, some sort of instructor.'*

'Probably a Rememberer.' He reacted to R'nemReth's confused look. *'It's common among primitive cultures who lack writing. The Remembers learn important tribal lore by rote, passing it down generation by generation.'*

She was amazed at the mental discipline that would take, which was all but beyond comprehension. *'That young one we contacted said he needed to speak with the Gray-Wing.'*

The uproar around them grew to a shrill thunder, catching their attention. R'nemReth tuned in to catch their thoughts. *'Why were these two not killed?'* one Flyer demanded. *'They sought to find our Aerie. Would you have them eat our eggs?'*

'The Gray-Wing insisted they be taken alive.' The White-Wing ruffled her wings menacingly. *'Do you question his Wisdom, Hunt-Leader?'*

There was an ugly silence as the assembled Flyers focussed on their confrontation. *'The Wisdom of the Gray-Wing is true.'* The Hunt-Leader's thoughts were sullen. *'Yet he lies here before us, stricken by the Sky-Faller's claws. Can his Wisdom save him?'*

'He's hurt!' K'nidMin's aura was not happy. There was a bright streak of blood on the fallen Flyer's wing. *'He must have been hit when they came to the camp. This doesn't look good.'*

R'nemReth focused on the broad smear of bright red blood. Inspiration came when it was needed most. "Can we help him?" she asked.

K'nidMin turned to her in surprise. "What do you mean?"

"This could be our chance. If we can save him, it may save our own lives."

'The lowlands by the big water have always been our feeding ground.' The Hunt-Leader shrill cries evoked a chorus of agreement. *'Long have we fought against the other Aeries to protect our herds. Now these creatures fall from the sky to extend claws to us, claiming our feeding grounds. This we cannot accept! We must meet them claw for claw!'*

"Great," K'nidMin grumbled. "This is what I was afraid of."

"Are they going to attack the camp?"

"It looks like it. These are top predators; they aren't about to sit meekly by when their very existence is threatened."

'They land on our feeding ground and walk around like common game, and I treated them as game!' the Hunt-Leader boasted. *'I matched claw with claw! I killed and ate one of them!'*

"R'nemReth, broadcast my thoughts," K'nidMin said, urgently. *'And you were sick afterward, weren't you?'* he thought.

The White-Wing and the others came to an abrupt, stunned silence and stared at them in amazement. Then she emitted a loud, multi-toned warble; her thought came at the same time. *'It speaks to us, but we do not hear its words?'*

'I have the power to speak from our minds to yours', R'nemReth answered. *'Hear me so we can prevent more deaths.'*

Hunt-Leader turned to them angrily. *'That one is not of the wings! It does not speak when the Aerie gathers!'*

'You were sick,' K'nidMin insisted. *'No one can eat meat proteans from an alien biosphere. We cannot eat your game any more than you could eat us.'* That caused a stir among the Flyers. He stepped into the open circle and gestured to the Hunt-Leader. *'So, you see, we are not poaching on your food stocks. This one is mistaken. He killed unjustly.'*

'This one is not of our Aerie! Its words have no meaning!'

K'nidMin confronted him. *'Have you seen any of us kill your food animals? Speak the truth before your Law!'*

There was a tense silence before the Hunt-Leader reluctantly admitted, *'I have not.'*

143

K'nidMin turned to the White-Wing. *'Then I say to you all the deaths on both sides are unjust. The original landing were explorers. They did not know this is your world; they mistook your attackers for dangerous animals and defended themselves. Those who came since seek to end this conflict and make peace.'*

'And yet when we came to you, you extended claws again!' Hunt-Leader said. *'Your words are false!'*

'The one who attacked you the other day was afraid; do not allow his fear to poison the peace. We wish to end this conflict. That is why we came here.'

R'nemReth was still shaky from her harrowing trip, and it made her impatient for him to get to the point. She tottered unevenly into the circle next to him and gestured at the Gray-Wing. *'Speaking of deaths, this one is hurt. He may die if his wound is not treated. Let us help him. It will show you the Truth of our words.'*

The White-Wing's skepticism was obvious. *'Why would you do this when it was your kind which harmed him?'*

R'nemReth fought down her near panic. *'It was a mistake. One of the humans...the tall ones...was stricken by fear when you approached our camp. We hoped to speak with you that day, but his actions drove you away.'*

"R'nemReth..."

She confronted the White-Wing, struggling to keep her thoughts steady. *'Let us treat his wound. We can save his life, and it will show you our good faith.'*

'We fly through strange weather; strange weather indeed.' She could sense the White-Wing's confusion and uncertainty. *'We cannot lose the Gray-Wing. His fledgling is not ready.'*

'Then let us save him.'

"I hope you know what you're doing," K'nidMin muttered as they examined the Gray-Wing's injury. The rest of the Aerie were eerily silent, watching. "If we can't save him now, we'll be eaten for sure!"

She avoided looking at all those huge mouths filled with sharp, pointed teeth. "We're on the menu anyway. You're the first aid expert, so what do we do?"

"*p'quas'tka* if I know," he mumbled, then started digging through his aid kit.

R'nemReth stared at the bloody wound, mesmerized by the gruesome sight, then turned to the Gray-Wing's left eye, which was watching them. *'This will hurt,'* she thought.

'Pain is nothing,' his thoughts came to her. *'Your words must be heard by the Aerie.'*

'You ordered them to spare us!'

'Yes. You must prevent a Clash of Aeries. Your claws are too sharp for us to endure.'

She and K'nidMin exchanged bemused looks; Young-Seeker's message was received after all. *'We'll do what we can.'*

K'nidMin clambered onto the wing and probed it carefully, evoking an occasional grunt of pain from the Gray-Wing. The wound, mercifully, was a simple through-and-through right where the left wing joined to the body. There was a lot of blood, and he soon spotted a severed artery. "That has to be tied off," he said.

R'nemReth was already digging through her first aid kit. "There aren't any sutures in this thing."

"Those kits don't have them." His ears sagged, momentarily stumped. "What can we use for sutures?"

"We can't put a tourniquet on it, can we?"

K'nidMin pondered the gushing wound for a moment, then glanced at her. "Clever! You might look at a career in medicine after this is over!"

"No, thank you," she grumbled. "What do you think?"

"Give me your kit." She handed it over, and he sorted the large adhesive patch out of it and from his kit. "Get me a couple short pieces of wood about as thick as your finger; a bit of tree branch will do."

While she scuttled around looking for something, he drew his utility knife, punched two holes in the centers of the patches, then carefully cut a length off the hem of his over-tunic. By time she returned, he was already washing the blood away from the wound.

"Here. This is all I could find."

He hesitated, then took the two small bones she found. "I hope these aren't human bones," he mumbled.

145

"They aren't, unless there are humans five lengths long."

He pondered the bones, bemused, then set to work. "I'm pioneering a new medical technique." He showed her his handiwork. "We'll call it a 'K'nidMin patch'."

"Wonderful. I hope we live to tell about it." At least they were doing something, which helped her jitters.

"I'll need your help. You need to get under the wing." He threaded the strip of cloth through one of the self-adhesive patches. "I'll pass this through the hole to you. You stick it through your patch, loop it around the bone, then back through the hole again. I'll tie it off and wind it up to apply pressure on that artery."

That *was* clever. "You're sure this'll work?" she asked, doubtfully.

"It better." He pondered the injury again. "We'll need to risk using disinfectant on the wound." He dug up the two packets of antiseptic powder and tore them open. "You know what to do? Let's get this done."

§

She was not thrilled as she crawled under the Gray-Wing's wing. The ground was muddy and soaked in blood, the space was claustrophobic, and there was a heavy animal smell. *'Can you stop the bleeding?'* the Gray-Wing's thought came as her nerves were starting to give way.

That helped steady her. *'I don't know, but I'd say the chances are good.'* She reached the spot where a steady trickle of blood dribbled. The Gray-Wing lost a lot of blood over the last several days; only his bulk had kept him alive thus far, and given them some hope of saving him. *'This is likely to hurt.'*

'I sing your praise,' his thought came in reply.

'Thank you.' She scrunched into place and called, "I'm ready!"

It was some time before anything happened, and she was about to call K'nidMin to see what the hangup was when a short piece of twig poked through the bullet hole, followed by the end of the cloth strip. The delay was him trying to improvise a needle. A gush of blood came with it, spattering her snout and hands. "*l'cc'vn,*" she muttered as she drew the strip out and threaded it through the patch after removing the backing paper.

146

Then she realized there was a problem: there was too much blood; the adhesive on the patch would be ruined. After a moment's confusion, she used the only thing she had to wipe the blood away; her sleeve. "Damn-fool way to make a living," she grumbled as she hastily stuck the twig through the hole again and pressed the patch home.

A moment later, K'nidMin drew the strip taut, and the wounded area slowly contracted as he applied pressure. "Let me know when the bleeding stops!" he yelled.

'I can hear you,' she thought, testily. It took several more turns on the cloth strip accompanied by a few grunts of pain from the Gray-Wing before the bleeding slowly ended.

§

"You do *NOT* know how to show a fem a good time!" she snapped at K'nidMin after crawling out from under the wing again. She was muddy, soaked in blood, chilled, and shaking from reaction.

"You look lovely," K'nidMin assured her. "Muddy brown is your color." She was a gory mess, in fact.

"Did it do any good?" she asked after venting her upset in some unprintable suggestions about his ancestry.

K'nidMin studied the patch. "The bleeding has stopped. It depends on how much blood he lost." He turned to the Gray-Wing. *'How do you feel?'*

'It is painful, but I can bear it. I sing your praise for trying to help me.'

"Now what?" she asked.

"Now we see." K'nidMin confronted the White-Wing again.

§

They were ignored for some time as the Flyers erupted in a thunderous argument, seemingly all shouting at once. Even the Gray-Wing lifted his head to shriek out a few comments.

'What are they doing?' K'nidMin thought. The volume was so great they had to cover their ears.

'I can't follow them. There are too many voices going way too fast.'

'Can you get any overall impressions?'

147

She focussed on the overwhelming storm of emotions and images. *'There...is much anger...much debate. They're really upset about something, but I can't tell what.'*

'Hopefully not us.'

The argument went on for some time until the White-Wing rose and spread her wings. The debate cut off abruptly, leaving a ringing silence. There was a brief, uncomfortable calm as the White-Wing pondered the scene around them, particularly the Gray-Wing and the two Ic'nichi. *'We have heard the words of the Hunt-Leader and the Sky-Fallers,'* she said at last. *'The wings will now decide.'*

"They were holding a trial," K'nidMin muttered.

"A trial? For who?"

K'nidMin's aura was chilly. "We'll find out soon enough."

§

It took some time for the White-Wing to question each Flyer there in turn and receive an answer. It was all brief, formal, and direct; a distinct change from the earlier chaos. The two Ic'nichi tried to follow the discussion, but it was little more than a roll call as the Flyers voted one by one. Eventually the roll was complete, and the White-Wing spoke.

'Hunt-Leader, the Aerie has heard the words of you and the Sky-Fallers. Hear now the true words of the Aerie. The Sky-Fallers have not taken any of our herds, nor can we eat them, so we must assume they cannot eat our herds as they said. Given these facts, you extended claws to them unjustly!'

'The kill I took was an intruder! We have ever battled those who trespass in our sky. Why should they be any different?'

'By the words of the Sky-Fallers, the one you took did not know of our kind, so they could not know our customs. We cannot bind someone to our Law if they do not even know we exist.'

'Their claws are sharp! Even if the one who died was innocent, they are a danger to us!'

'And your answer to this is a clash of Aeries with the Sky-Fallers when they would retract claws? This can only lead to many more folded wings!'

'How can we believe the words of those not our kind?'

148

'They came to us at risk of death to speak soft words. They use their powers to aid the Gray-Wing. By their acts their words are true.'

There was a brief, tense silence save for the whisper of the wind and the rustling of many enormous wings. For once it seemed Hunt-Leader had no answer.

'Hunt-Leader, hear now the Speaking of Law.' the White-Wing intoned. *'The death of the Sky-Faller was a tragic mistake. Due to your act, three respected Hunters of the Aerie have died, and the Sky-Fallers are filled with anger so the Aerie itself is in danger.'*

K'nidMin and R'nemReth exchanged bemused looks, hardly daring to believe what they were hearing.

'You have created a problem which no Speaking of Law has ever dealt with in all the Time of Legends,' the White-Wing went on. *'New Law must be spoken for this, so we must backwing to the principle of duty to the Aerie. Since you have jeopardized the Aerie, so you shall be stripped of your role as Hunter and cast out. And you shall evermore be known as Black-Wing!'*

There was a collective gasp from the Aerie gathered around as the ex-Hunter's head and wings drooped in shame. *'What happened?'*

The Gray-Wing looked around, and saw K'nidMin looking at him. *'He is outcast. He is dishonored by the Aerie, and may never fly in our sky again on pain of death.'*

'Black-Wing,' the White-Wing's thought was cold and formal. *'You are banned from the sky. You have until dark to leave this air forever. From first light, to enter this air is death!'*

'Indeed?' K'nidMin thought.

§

After Black-Wing flew away, the Aerie turned their attention to them. *'We fly through strange weather,'* the White-Wing thoughts followed her warbling screech. *'Never has the Aerie flown such skies in all the Time of Legends. These Sky-Fallers are not of us, yet they are clearly reasoning beings who bear their own Light. They are not of the Aeries, yet they are not for feeding. What are they? This we must decide.'*

"This is it," K'nidMin muttered as the tension rose.

'We must backwing to the good of the Aerie,' someone's thought came. *'The Sky-Fallers bring strange powers and sharp claws which strike at a distance. Many have felt those claws already. Do they pose a threat to the Aerie? This we must decide.'* That brought on a shrill chorus of responses.

The Gray-Wing struggled to his feet; the chorus died down as they focussed on him. *'It is true they bring sharp claws, yet it was the Black-Wing who took the first prey.'* His aura was filled with pain, yet his thought carried firm resolve. *'It is we who showed claws to them! It is we who should speak our Truth, not them!'*

'Are you alright?' R'nemReth asked since he looked pretty wobbly.

The Gray-Wing turned to them with some difficulty. *'I live. There is Wisdom to be spoken, as is my duty.'* He turned to address the Aerie. *'The Sky-Fallers come to us to retract claws. They used their strange powers to stop my bleeding and they speak soft words to us. This shows us their Truth.'*

'They strike and speak as one,' someone thought. *'How can their words be true?'*

'The one who struck at you was afraid,' K'nidMin thought. *'He is now Black-Wing among us, and will be sent back to his world in disgrace.'*

'The riddle is answered,' the Gray-Wing addressed the White-Wing. *'The dishonor of one cannot condemn all, by your own Speaking of Law.'*

'This is Wisdom.' The White-Wing pondered for a time, then turned her attention to the two Ic'nichi. *'What are your true words? What do you seek in our sky?'*

K'nidMin spoke up promptly. *'We wish to retract our claws. We wish to make a Speaking of Law to end this conflict. We wish to have peace between our three races.'*

'There are two kinds of Sky-Fallers,' someone thought. *'What do the others, the tall ones, say? Can you speak for them?'*

'We came here to work together to solve this problem,' K'nidMin thought. *'There are officials...Elders...at our camp who speak for our two races. They bear the Law of our kind, and have the power to make a Speaking of Law to resolve this crisis.'*

'And yet these First Sky-Fallers did not come with you." The White-Wing's tone was suspicious. 'How can you speak for all when they do not come here?'

'We came without them since they have twice harmed your people. It was a tragic mistake, as you said yourself, but we feared you would not speak with us if they came along.'

The White-Wing's thought grew chill. 'So you violated your Law to come here? How can your words be true, then?'

K'nidMin's aura was suddenly filled with tension. R'nemReth felt his uncertainty as he froze in confusion.

'How can we believe your words when you violate your own Law?' the White-Wing demanded.

"This...isn't working," he mumbled. He was stuck, and the Flyers were growing impatient.

Inspiration and her street smarts came to the rescue. 'Our Aeries are vast and our Law cannot answer everyone's needs,' she thought. 'Some of us, under certain conditions, must use our own initiative to tell what the true words are.'

'What is this?' The White-Wing's aura was confused. 'How can one be granted exception from Law?'

'As you said just a while ago, sometimes the Speaking of Law can't provide answers. We improvise when we have to.'

'Yet you made Law for this place, then violated your Law by coming here alone. How can your words be true?'

R'nemReth gave it her best shot with a prayer to her Ancestors for guidance. 'Our Law did not anticipate this when Law was spoken. When Law cannot help us we have to create new Law on the spot for the greater good.'

There was a brief, uncomfortable silence as the White-Wing pondered. K'nidMin looked at R'nemReth in dismay, his aura a mix of embarrassment and relief. "Fast thinking," he muttered.

"Not fast enough to get me out of trouble the last time."

'We have heard your words,' the White-Wing thought at last. 'The wings will now decide.'

*****

151

"A Meeting Of Minds"

They could hear the general alarm shrieking even before they arrived at Fort Zinderneuf, and could see tiny figures scrambling to the gun positions. *'You better land here, out of range,'* K'nidMin thought.

The Hunters carrying them backwinged, hovered not far from the landing pad, and released them—at perhaps three lengths' altitude. "Ow!" R'nemReth cried as she landed in a heap. *"p'quas'tka!"*

"Are you alright?" K'nidMin asked as he helped her to her feet.

"No, I am *not* alright," she grumbled. "I *hate* flying! Those claws half squeezed my innards out of me, I'm cold and wet and hungry, and I've got an *Ancestorless* headache!"

"Ah! It's good to see you're back to your old self."

She gave K'nidMin a scathing look as the rest of the Aerie settled around them in a broad rank around the camp just out of machine gun range. "I'd have your ears, but then there'd be nothing left of you!"

He laughed at her discomfiture. "Probably so. Come on; we need to get this done before some *n'bna'nmn* panics and starts shooting again."

§

Lieutenant Horton was waiting for them as they came limping back to camp. "Thank God! We thought you were dead!"

"We had a little adventure," K'nidMin said. "But we're back, and we have good news."

"I hope you do." Horton gestured at the massed ranks of Flyers who all but surrounded them. "That doesn't look good out there."

"Well you can relax. We talked with their Elders and ironed out the original misunderstanding. All that remains now is to negotiate a formal treaty."

"Great! Now we'll get some use out of Sir Miles."

K'nidMin's Worthy was there as well. "Glad to have you back. Sir Miles is wetting himself over you going off like that, and G'nemBrik is having second thoughts all round. You better watch your tail in there."

152

"And Perncroft's having a hissy-fit," Horton added. "He intends to nail your hide to the barn door."

"He does, eh? We'll see about that! As for the show out there, we'll light a fire under Sir Miles' tail. Like you said, it's time to get some use out of him."

"I sincerely *hope* so. We won't last long if that lot decides to attack."

§

Sir Miles was, in fact, on the verge of hysterics when they came into the admin grotto. "What have you done?!" he cried. "Are we going to be attacked? What are they planning?"

K'nidMin was in a surly mood by then, and got all ears-forward with him. "You can quit your *r'vebbe!* We solved the crisis *you* people created."

Captain Pencroft was there as well; dressed in combat fig, waving an assault rifle, and looking slightly hysterical. "This is *supposed* to be a joint mission!" he shouted. "Why did you go off on your own in direct violation of standing orders?"

"We had to since *your* people *repeatedly* poisoned any chance of making a breakthrough," K'nidMin shouted in turn. "The only thing we could do was go into their territory to prove how serious we were in contacting them, *without* bringing you humans due to your well-earned reputation for chasing your own tails!"

R'nemReth sensed Pencroft crumbling under K'nidMin's attack. *'We put our lives on the line,'* she thought, forcefully. *'And we got results; results you humans made all but impossible!'*

Pencroft twitched all over. "Damn you, madam, must you do that? Why can't you learn our language so we can talk like civilized people?"

"We don't have time for this," K'nidMin said. "We have more *urgent* priorities than *your* discomfort!"

Arbiter G'nemBrik stepped in to quell the rising tone. "You have results? What have you achieved?"

K'nidMin fought down his temper. "We were captured and taken to their Aerie. They had a huge debate over whether to attack this camp. *Her* telepathy made it possible to talk them out of it and straighten out the misunderstanding which caused this mess. The one who killed the human was banished, and they came here at *our* invitation to negotiate a treaty." He glared at the two diplomats. "Now, are you going to make a liar out of me and get this camp overrun, or are you going out there to meet with them?" He crossed his arms and waited for their answer.

§

"Couldn't we at least get something to eat before coming out here again?" R'nemReth muttered plaintively to K'nidMin as they trudged out into the prairie.

"Sorry. We have the initiative for the moment, but we don't dare lose it."

"We need to get a move-on," Horton said. "Pencroft was beating the war drums big-time while you were absent. Our people are seriously on edge."

In fact K'nidMin's Worthy and Sergeant MacIntosh were riding tight herd on the human peacekeepers, with the 'Dark Grays' mixed in among them to prevent any more 'accidents'. Captain Pencroft was livid at this interference with his command, but was under strict orders from Sir Miles not to 'do anything stupid'. Thus far anyway he hadn't gained much traction, but none of them wanted to give him time to wiggle out of his restraints.

"Do you think we can forge a treaty?" Horton asked as they drew closer to the Flyers. The sight of all those enormous creatures standing upright on their haunches with their wings spread was unnerving.

"They're willing to listen, but they don't normally negotiate with other Aeries, and we have some selling to do after all the bloodshed." K'nidMin pondered the White-Wing, just ahead, then added, "It can be done, but we better not blow it this time."

He was right about that, as reluctant as R'nemReth was to admit it. The collective aura of the Flyers was chill and reserved; their upright posture a potent threat display. It would take a lot of selling to bring them around; it wouldn't take much to push them away.

The afternoon was made for their mindset. The sky was overcast with the approach of another storm, a brisk wind chilled them, and it was sprinkling off and on. Wading through the underbrush soaked their legs by time they reached the landing pad, where they made their stand.

Arbiter G'nemBrik and Sir Miles hesitated when they confronted the Flyer elders. "Ah, R'nemReth, will you make introductions all round, please?" G'nemBrik asked.

'This is the White-Wing,' she introduced their leader. *'She is the tribal elder and the Speaker of Law.'* The White-Wing rustled her wings in a formal greeting, which nearly *r'vebbe'd* Sir Miles. *'And this is the Gray-Wing, their Keeper of Legends. He is a sort of record keeper and teacher of the young.'*

"Is that an injury?" Arbiter G'nemBrik pointed to the bandage on the Gray-Wing's left wing.

"Yes, sir," K'nidMin said. "That's a bullet wound from their last visit here. We were able to contain some severe bleeding, which may have saved his life."

"Good work on that," Lieutenant Holden muttered.

'And these are our Elders,' R'nemReth introduced them to the Flyers in turn. *'Arbiter G'nemBrik, of our people, and Ambassador Sir Miles Willoughby for the humans.'*

'These two are your Bringers of Law?' the White-Wing demanded.

'They are. They come bearing the authority of our leaders to speak Law to settle the dispute between us.'

The White-Wing's aura was chill and severe. She pondered the two delegates for some time, looking back and forth between them. *'We will hear your words,'* she thought at last.

§

And so formal negotiations began. There was no practical option for the Concord party other than to set up on the landing pad with some folding chairs and thermal blankets as their only creature comforts. The Flyers promptly moved in to surround the negotiating party on all sides, which nearly *r'vebbe'd* Sir Miles again, although Arbiter G'nemBrik correctly recognized it as a negotiating tactic.

It turned out the Flyers were cunning negotiators. They would frequently get into one of their screeching debates while still surrounding them, which left the negotiators' ears ringing. They were uncompromising, arbitrary, switched topics constantly, and only begrudgingly gave concessions with much screeching and flapping of wings. Another trick they employed was for their hunters to take several herd beasts which they consumed in a gory spectacle where the negotiating party couldn't help but see. Arbiter G'nemBrik and Sir Miles were soon reduced to a state as the White-Wing and her cohorts kept up the constant pressure.

R'nemReth was kept busy as translator, probably the busiest and most challenging time of her life, and managed to offer occasional insights about the Flyer mindset and negotiating strategy.

K'nidMin and Horton remained with her for moral support when the others were sent back to the camp, but the pace was too hectic for her to fret. The negotiations dragged on through the morning and into midday, and at times it seemed progress was impossible. Only R'nemReth's telepathic power, which allowed her to sniff out the Flyers' mindset, allowed the negotiators to advance the cause.

§

"I'll be thankful when this is done and we can get off this *l'cc'vn* world!" R'nemReth grumbled. They were taking a brief break at the moment while the politicians and Flyers argued among themselves in two separate groups. "I am sick to death of this endless wind!"

She, K'nidMin and Horton were in their own huddle, mostly sharing war stories and complaints about the weather. "How long do you think this nonsense will go on?" Horton asked.

"It's hard to say," K'nidMin said. "I can tell you from experience the Flyers love to argue, but once they make up their minds, they get it done." He pondered the diplomats in a huddle on the coveted metal landing pad, the driest spot available. "Things can break any time."

"Do you think we'll get a treaty?"

"Hopefully. The Flyers are afraid of our 'distant claws', but it will depend on how stupid the 'brains' are."

"God help us!" she sighed.

§

The negotiations adjourned late in the day, and the diplomatic party trudged back to the camp where K'nidMin's Worthy and Sergeant MacIntosh greeted them. "So how are things here?" Horton asked. "Everything under control?"

"Aye, things are quiet enough, as the troops ha' seen our people palavering wi' yon beasties," MacIntosh said. "How goes that, sir?"

"We're making progress," she mumbled. "It's not over yet."

'I wish they'd get it done!' R'nemReth thought. *'That wind is driving me er'trxxda!'*

"If the cold is botherin' ye, lassie, try a wee drop o' this." MacIntosh drew a bottle out of his kit and handed it to her. "It'll make a Scotsman out of ye!"

She unwisely took a slug, then gasped as her ill-considered drink exploded in her innards. *'Ancestors! What was that?!'*

"Tis a fine single malt, an' ye quaffed it like a true Scot."

'I...thought...that wasn't 'sti'eit!'

"'sti'eit?" MacIntosh gave a snort of contempt. "Fine for polishing buttons, that, but nay a proper drink." To emphasize the point, he took a hearty swig from the bottle in turn.

§

The Flyers remained where they were overnight, ringing the camp, and keeping up a steady racket of hooting and screeching which had everyone on edge.

The next morning brought more of the same—after a sleepless night, and with the added annoyance of a new weather system to dampen the proceedings. The Flyers held the added advantage that if the negotiations failed, they had Fort Zinderneuf surrounded and at close range. The Concord party was painfully aware that failure was not an option.

Despite the Flyers' ploys, the renewed rain, and various 'stupidity', they hammered out a basic agreement after a day and a half of negotiations.

"Ancestors! I hope I don't have to go through *that* again!" Arbiter G'nemBrik sighed as they trudged back to the camp.

"One hopes," Sir Miles grumbled. "But it was worth it, I suppose."

The gist of the formal treaty between the Flyers and the Concord was their recognition that the Flyers were an intelligent species with rights the star-traveling races had to respect, and that they were the rightful owners of this world with complete authority to decide who came there and under what circumstances. In return the Flyers allowed Fort Zinderneuf to remain as a contact point provided the visitors did not expand it or interfere with the grazing herds the Flyers depended on for food. Scientific and cultural expeditions beyond the coastal plain into Flyer territory would be allowed on a case by case basis. The Flyers agreed to allow representatives of other Aeries to enter their air to visit the camp. Finally the original human death and the three Flyers killed were marked off as a 'regrettable misunderstanding'. Having clearly established it was *they* who called the shots on this world, the Flyers made a surprisingly fair treaty.

"It's hardly a comprehensive document," G'nemBrik said. "There are still matters of trade, cultural exchange, conflict resolution and a whole lot more to work out."

"Which are matters for others to agonize over," Sir Miles grumbled. "I pity the *next* poor fool they send here. I have had my fill of this wet, miserable world, thank you very much!"

As to emphasize the point, a burst of wind ruffled their overcoats as a renewed rain squall drummed on their heads, causing them to cower and curse. "Ancestors," G'nemBrik muttered. "I'll resign from the Arbiters if they try to saddle me with another stellar assignment!"

§

"This is fascinating," Doctor Lassiter said as the Contact Herd reviewed the result. "The negotiation methods of true alpha predators are nothing less than extraordinary!"

"I doubt our diplomats share your admiration," Learnéd C'venBren replied, which got a relieved chuckle from everyone. "We've learned some valuable lessons from this experience, which we need to share all round as soon as possible."

"Especially the lesson about the value of a telepath," Learnéd Z'gehRoo added. "R'nemReth was not only a valuable translator, but allowed us to spy on the Flyers at the same time."

"I'd swear we caught the White-Wing off guard more than once," K'nidMin said. He gave her a grateful ear twitch and a big grin. "You did it; more than we hoped for. I think it's fair to say you made this treaty possible."

Their praise and approval, and her own real sense of accomplishment made her feel good about herself for the first time in a long time.

§

There was a celebration for the new compact in the cafeteria that evening, but K'nidMin and R'nemReth slipped out after a brief obligatory appearance. Both of them were tired, and simply wanted some time alone with their thoughts.

"You can be proud of what we accomplished," K'nidMin said as they shared a can of *l'ni'ddi* warmed over a gas-burning heater. "We managed to save the situation, not to mention the first real accomplishment for our herd, due in no small part to you."

"Yes, well, I saved our lives as well, don't forget. We wouldn't stand a chance if the Flyers attack this place."

K'nidMin's aura changed to admiration. "True. You were the key to it all."

The renewed rain drowned out their words, and they huddled together under the open awning of the lookout perch where they sought a bit of privacy. *'Miserable place,'* she thought. The vast emptiness of the coastal plain stretched as far as they could see in the dim light. There were no lights anywhere out there. It emphasized how far they were from anything, and gave her a desolate feeling.

'I've seen better.' K'nidMin stoked up the portable heater used to cook their *l'ni'ddi*. The warmth of the flame and the aromatic steam were a reassuring touch. *'I won't miss this weather.'*

The rain squall passed after a short while, leaving a damp chill with patchy fog. "So what happens now?" she asked as he warmed some instant *V'liz*.

K'nidMin handed her a steaming bowl and pondered her question. "I suppose we'll return to d'enchia. I'll put in a good report on your efforts, as I'm sure Arbiter G'nemBrik will, and you should get that Writ of Forbearance."

159

"What about my psychic powers? That was what led to all my problems to begin with. It won't do me any good to go home if I'm still saddled with them."

"Good point." K'nidMin mused on it. "I suppose we can ask J J Ballas to remove them."

"Well ah can do that if you like." They looked up, startled, to see J J Ballas standing by the railing. "But then, maybe you ought t' think on keepin' them instead, Lil-Missy."

"*Keep them?* Why would I do that? I want to live a normal life, thank you!"

"Ah can understand that," J J said. "But them powers have a lasting effect on th' mind. You was hatched wit' the empath, an' yo' mind won't be complete without it."

Coming from him, that was ominous. "What do you mean 'won't be complete'?"

"Them powers saturate all through yo' mind. Th' longer they in there, the harder it is t' yank 'em out again. Yo' parents only had their powers fo' a short time, and they needed a lot of tinkering when we removed 'em. Ah can take back the telepath right enough, but the empath is too deep in yo' mind." They both felt a chill aura from him. "Tryin' t' remove it now would be bad; real bad."

"So I'm doomed, thanks to you!"

J J mused on that. "It depends on how you look on it. You got a rare gift an' you could do some real good with it."

"I'd like to give *you* a 'rare gift'!"

J J chuckled, which flooded them with a light-hearted aura. "You know, yo' sure remind me of yo' ma, yo mother, when she was young." He glanced at K'nidMin. "She a might temperamental 'un, ain't she?"

"I'd say 'spirited' is probably a better term," K'nidMin said, judiciously.

"Or the wiser, anyway." J J chuckled again. "In any case, ah can take back the telepath if you want, but it gives you a special talent you could do some good with." He gave her that one-eyed blink. "You think on it, Lil-Missy. Ol' J J will be listening." He vanished again.

"I swear we could go to the ends of the galaxy and not find people as strange as them," K'nidMin muttered as he stirred the *V'liz* some more.

'I'm not sure I'd want to,' she thought.

§

It was five more days before the human patrol ship returned and arrangements were made to take the Contact Herd to Checkpoint. "This'll be a crowded trip," Horton grumbled. The two teams, thirteen total, were a huge load for a destroyer. "We'll be stacked like cordwood in the cargo hold, like we were last time."

"Yes, but we're headed for Checkpoint, so I'd say the trip was worth it," Learnéd C'venBren said.

"You got that right!" Horton paused and watched a group of Flyers circling in the distance. "I'll kind of miss this," she sighed. "The Flyers aren't such a bad sort after all." It turned out the Flyers' predatory instincts were a good match for her martial personality, once they got to know each other.

"Well I, for one, am happy to get out of here!" K'nidMin added a snort of frustration. "I just wonder how things will go without our telepath around to help out."

"Yes, well, that's up to the linguists and xenosociologists now. At least they won't have to worry about Pencroft. I hear Sir Miles lowered the boom on him after his fear-mongering almost blew up on us." In fact, Captain Pencroft was standing off to one side looking a bit lost. He was headed back to earth, relived of duty by Sir Miles, and the gossip was his career was finished.

"My hearts cry for him," K'nidMin grumbled. "Look out: here comes the shuttle."

The shuttle's landing brought the Flyers soaring in, curious to see what was going on. They circled overhead for a while as some cargo was unloaded and the passengers boarded. Curiosity satisfied, they drifted away one by one until only Young-Seeker was left.

'Good bye, Young-Seeker,' R'nemReth thought as they were about to board the shuttle.

'You go to your Aerie?' he thought in turn.

'Yes, we return to where we belong.'

He circled overhead around the grounded shuttle as last minute preparations were being made. *'You are welcome to fly with me.'*

R'nemReth was touched. *'Thank you, Young-Seeker. Maybe someday I will.'*

They paused to watch as Young-Seeker drifted away, his broad wings riding the thermals along the coast. "I'd be tempted to take him up on that offer some day," Horton muttered.

She didn't say anything, but privately she felt the same.

*****

"The Far Horizon"

Another ten days in weightlessness brought them back to Checkpoint. It turned out ship 200 wasn't due from earth for three days yet, so they took the shuttle down.

The weather was warm, as always; a welcome change from the Flyers' world. "Ancestors, this feels good!" K'nidMin said as they trudged toward the encampment. "Cold and wet is not my favorite pastime. I'm looking forward to spending a few days relaxing on the beach."

R'nemReth was distracted by a feeling which seemed off. "Something's changed," she said as she eyed the buildings ahead of them. "Something is different." She could sense the faint psychic white noise of the multitude...but above it were a host of clean, pinpoint bright thoughts which seemed familiar...

K'nidMin stopped and looked at her in confusion. "What?"

Then she realized she was hearing the Li-qua's minds. She could sense them clearly, like glittering stars in the night sky. "Something happened to the Li-qua. They're not the same. I can hear their thoughts."

"It could be your telepathy is improving with practice."

"Maybe." She wasn't convinced. "But I don't think so. They've changed somehow."

Just then they spotted Loo-loo-ba scuttling toward them. *'Howdy, K'nidMin. Howdy, R'nemReth. It's good t' have you back. Our hut is empty for both of you.'*

K'nidMin studied Loo-loo-ba in confusion. "J J? Did you give him telepathy?"

The next thing they knew, J J Ballas was there, as large as life and emitting a smug aura. "Well howdy Boss, an' you too, Lil-Missy. It's good t' see you-all again."

K'nidMin wasn't put off by his hale-fellow-well-met routine. "You gave him telepathy, didn't you?"

"Ah did that," J J said, thoughtfully. "You'ah experience wit' her got me t' thinkin'. Ah took a good close look at his mind, an' he's got what it takes, so ah gifted him with it. It's been a big help t' them."

'Yes,' Loo-loo-ba added. *'Now that we can communicate with you-all, we've made some real progress. The adaptation project is goin' strong, our population is rising, an' we're feelin' a whole lot better 'bout th' future.'*

"It's not just him." R'nemReth gave J J a suspicious glare. "You did it to all of them, didn't you?"

'He sho' did.' Loo-loo-ba's thoughts bubbled with pleasure. *'He done good fo' us.'*

R'nemReth couldn't help giggle. "He's imitating you, J J!"

J J emitted an aura of embarrassment. "Yeah. They all do it."

'So when are you two gonna take the plunge?' Loo-loo-ba asked.

K'nidMin gave her a quizzical look. "You have me there. I'm not sure how to answer that one."

R'nemReth flushed in embarrassment. "We aren't going to be taking any *'plunges'*, thank you!"

"What was it you said about her, Boss?' J J's aura was amused. "Strong-willed an' self-reliant, ah think it was."

K'nidMin's ears reclined in chagrin. "Um...something like that."

R'nemReth had neither the time nor the patience for awkward conversation. "So what about my telepathy? What are you going to do about it now that the mission is over?"

J J mused for a bit. "Strictly speakin' ah ought t' remove it, the sooner the better. But then, you handled it well, an' they's plenty of things could be done with it, if yo' want to."

That put R'nemReth in a fix. The empathy she was saddled with made her life miserable; her big fear all along was what telepathy would do to her. But now that she was familiar with it, her telepathy wasn't so dreadful. There were advantages to it in fact, which she would be foolish to give up—if the long term risk wasn't too great. She would miss Loo-loo-ba's clear, incisive thoughts, too.

"This telepathy will alter my mind, won't it? Like the empathy I was hatched with?" she asked J J.

"It will eventually, but they ain't no big rush about it. You could go fo' a time wit'out it affecting you none."

"What will it do to me?"

J J mused some more, eying her speculatively. "You might say it's addictive. It won't drive you crazy or nothin', but you'll get t' where you'll be lost wit'out it."

That didn't sound so bad if she was willing to take the powers which went with it. Her telepathy gave her a powerful edge which could make a big difference in the struggle for that Writ of Forbearance. As concerned as she was about it affecting her (which was less of a worry, now she thought about it) she would be foolish to cast it aside until she knew what awaited her on d'enchia.

"I guess...maybe we could hold off for a while." She turned to K'nidMin. "You mentioned about helping the Arbiters; perhaps I should keep these powers for now, just in case they're needed."

"Just in case they're needed back home too, hmm?" J J gave her a jaundiced look. "Like maybe figurin' yo way past yo father?"

She flushed with embarrassment while K'nidMin chuckled. "The Ki-Elder may already be outclassed," he said.

"Maybe so, between her and her ma." J J's aura radiated amusement. "Still, he owes her, and he's a stubborn cuss, so it wouldn't hurt fo' her t' have the edge, fo' now."

She already drew the same conclusion. "I guess...if it won't do me any harm in the short run, perhaps I should hold onto the telepathy for the time being."

J J gave K'nidMin a thoughtful look. "Well then, since there ain't no hurry, let's go wit' her feelin' on this."

With that, he vanished into thin air. *'Now there is one unusual alien,'* Loo-loo-ba thought.

§

The next three days were free of any obligations, any problems, any immediate worries. R'nemReth managed to put the future out of mind, and spent much of her days laying in the shade of some tall grass listening to the surf and enjoying the drowsy warmth.

Some humans spent their free time playing in the water, and she watched them idly. They would paddle out on large sculpted boards to where the surf began forming, then would ride in on the heavy swells. Most did poorly, falling off their boards, not that they didn't try again.

"Humans," she muttered in dismay. One human managed to keep his footing, riding the swell until he reached the beach amid the cheers of the others. *'That looks like fun.'* She was impressed in spite of herself, not that she would ever try it.

K'nidMin came by while the human was getting reorganized. For once he wasn't wearing gray issue fatigues, having switched to a short-sleeved tunic printed with gaudy flowers and a set of shorts which showed rather too much tail. "So how are you?"

"I'm fine, thank you." She eyed him curiously. "Is that a new uniform?"

"Hardly. This is an adaptation of some human tropical wear."

"It...suits you, somehow."

He offered an amused snort. "I'm just channeling my inner *t'pithm'ig*." After a moment, he asked, "Do you have any plans for this evening?"

"Nothing in particular. Why?"

He seemed a bit awkward. "Our people here have started a human tradition called a 'luau'. It's a big party on the beach with fires and singing and food. Would you like to go?"

She was surprised and flattered that he would actually invite her out on a date. "Yes...I'd like to. Thank you."

§

The Ic'nichi interpretation of a 'luau' was an interesting spectacle, to say the least. The evening was tropic warm, as always, and the tangy salt air was flavored with wood smoke and the scents of cooking. The beach was lit by two large bonfires and several solar lamps, and the party-goers squatted on a long row of blankets spread on the sand.

A great many of the locals were there, most dressed in wild attire and precious little of it. Several humans were there as well, notably Lieutenant Horton and Sergeant MacIntosh, who made a drunken, incoherent, bombastic speech which the crowd was drunk enough to cheer along at every pause.

The food was basic camp fare, but the banqueters from the commissary outdid themselves, creating *interesting* new variants on such basics as *bv'nunma* and *uf'thoka*. Appetites were helped along by generous amounts of liquid refreshment.

166

Many of the party-goers, including R'nemReth and K'nidMin, used the occasion to play in the surf. The cool tropic water was bracing, and she was able to forget her problems and enjoy the moment as they splashed and dunked each other. For the first time in a long time, she was able to relax and enjoy his company, leaving her worldly cares behind as they frolicked like two hatchlings.

Finally, as the party was starting to break up, they waded out of the surf and settled on the beach. "I wish this could go on forever," she sighed.

"I know what you mean." His aura was somber, and she could tell something was bothering him.

She turned to him. "What is it?"

He was silent for a moment, brooding. "The ship entered the system a few hours ago. They'll be in orbit by morning." He settled on the sand with a weary sigh. "All good things must come to an end, I guess."

§

At long last ship 200 arrived back at d'enchia. R'nemReth glued herself to the lounge window once again, watching the lovely blue and green world below with deep longing and deeper regret. As is, the only thing waiting for her there was arrest and a lifetime of imprisonment. Her old street instincts reasserted themselves, reminding her she was not safe yet, nor was she likely to be. She did her part and more, but she still had to depend on the Ki-Elder who resented the blood ties between them and had no reason to uphold his part of the bargain.

K'nidMin's herd took the shuttle down for a well earned release in the World Nest, while K'nidMin, his Worthy and her took the transit bug over to the orbital station. Like ship 200, the orbital station featured a rotating habitat and quarters for those shifting from one ship to another, although the accommodations were more like a barracks.

"It might be better if you stay here for now until I have the chance to scout around down there," K'nidMin said. "As long as you don't touch dirt, we can claim your mission isn't complete. In any case, if you go down, the authorities will have to take notice."

She wasn't going to dispute it. "How long until you'll know anything?" she asked.

"I'm not sure." He offered a comforting ear twitch; his area wasn't so reassuring. "Success is something new for us. My Worthy will remain here to provide you cover, and I'll make sure to keep you in the circle on what goes on down there."

Some time later, she watched from a viewport as his shuttle bit into atmosphere, and for the first time since she began her journey, she felt alone.

§

K'nidMin's Worthy looked in on her from time to time, usually finding her by the observation windows. "You're longing for home, aren't you?" he said on one such occasion.

"I don't have a home," she said, bitterly. "There's nothing I want down there."

"And yet you spend a lot of time staring out these windows." He settled opposite her. "There's some part of you still down there, something you left behind. Isn't there?"

"Only regrets."

He offered an introspective ear twitch. "We all have regrets, but you can't let them rule your life. The best thing to do is let go of the past and look to the future. That excess baggage only slows you down."

His words made good sense, and his aura radiated mature confidence in himself, although he wasn't much older than her. "Don't you miss your home?"

He pondered for a bit. "The Service becomes our home after a while," he said, philosophically. "We're all part of a close-knit herd with an important, demanding purpose. We depend on each other. We're closer to each other than any civilians could ever be. You get caught up in it." He sighed. "I sometimes wonder what I'll do with myself once I retire."

As she thought about it later, she envied him. He found something in the Service she never knew, something she only dreamed of in her lonely years on the street. It left her wondering what would become of her once the mission ended.

§

168

The next day she was called to the communications center, where the watch Elder told her there was a message from downside. "But keep it brief," he said. "This is an official channel, and we need to keep it clear for important traffic."

She took the call eagerly, hoping it was the Ki-Elder wanting to inform her that her Writ of Forbearance had come through. Instead it was C'traBenla. "I'm so grateful you are back home safe!" she said.

She managed to mask her disappointment: she'd forgotten her mother had the grunt to gain access to Fleet communications. "It was no fun. The Ki-Elder said it would be unpleasant, and he wasn't kidding."

"He was being honest with you, R'nemReth. But you did it. You solved the problem. I'm so proud of you!"

That felt good, but it didn't answer the pressing question. "Will he change his mind about me?"

"He better, if he knows what's good for him!"

"Mother...I would rather do this myself. I can handle him. Please don't get into a squabble over me."

There was a brief silence, then, "You have my temperament, youngling. It can be a challenge at times."

That tickled her. "Second Degree K'nidMin described me as 'Strong-willed and self-reliant'."

"Did he?" She had a curious set to her ears. "I've heard some good things about him. So...is he interested in you?"

"Mother!" She was embarrassed. "Actually...he has shown some interest from time to time, but it's nothing serious."

C'traBenla greeted that with a derisive snort. "That sort of thing is *always* serious, youngling. Still, from what I hear, you could do worse."

"Really, mother, this is not the time to get involved with anyone."

"That time comes when it comes, dear. It's not something you 'plan' for. Trust me: I know."

The watch Elder was giving her a chilly glare. She needed to keep on topic. "What about the Ki-Elder? Will he keep his promise?"

"He can be a stubborn *un'tdar* when it comes to his duty, but he was impressed by the report he received about the mission. He'll come around, in time."

"I hope he does. I did my part, and now it's his turn." The watch Elder's aura was smoldering. "I have to go, mother; the tail-shaker in residence is giving me nasty looks."

She snorted in contempt. "Just remind him whose hatchling you are. Good bye for now, dear. I hope to see you soon. And about K'nidMin, a word of advice: always keep him guessing."

§

K'nidMin returned after mid-meal two days later, and his aura bubbled with enthusiasm. "Well, mission accomplished, the reports are all in, and the Contact Herd racks up their first solid win. Word is we're to get a medallion, all round."

A medallion: an approving ear twitch from the tail-shakers. That may be a fine thing for career military types, but she had more immediate problems. "So what happens to me now?"

K'nidMin offered an optimistic ear twitch. "I wrote up a glowing report on your contribution to resolving the Flyer contact, as did Arbiter G'nemBrik. I also argued your case with the Ki-Elder, and I think I scored some points there. I'd say there's a good chance of you getting your Writ of Forbearance."

"You spoke with him? What did he say?"

K'nidMin's aura cooled somewhat. "As a matter of fact, he called me in for a personal interview. I told him you were instrumental in our success, and I consider you a valuable member of our herd. I'm not sure if he was impressed."

"Well, thank you for that," she said, softly. It felt good to have important people championing her cause, for all the good it would do. "But what happens if he doesn't come through?"

"By rights he should. It may take him some time to sort it out, but you can be optimistic."

She gave that a contemptuous ear twitch. "You've never been on the street, have you? 'Right' has nothing to do with it. He has what he wants, and he'll be just as happy to see me filed and forgotten."

His aura turned pessimistic. "Yes, well, there is that."

"You can't change his mind, can you?"

K'nidMin was ear-fallen. "I don't have anything like the grunt it would take to influence him." She hardly needed her powers to feel his embarrassment. "Look: I have some connections with the Arbiters. G'nemBrik will support you, and your abilities can be a big help to the diplomats. I'm sure they can twist some tails in the Chamber."

"Well...maybe..."

"But then, you know how top-heavy the bureaucracy is," K'nidMin added. "This could take years."

Her frustration was starting to get to her. "I'll fight this out until the Ancestors are sick of it! I'll appeal all the way to the Chamber if I have to! That *M'mendoch* made a promise, and I'll have his ears if he tries to wiggle out of it!"

'What was it you said about her, Boss?' J J's presence echoed. *'Strong-willed an' self-reliant, ah think it was.'*

K'nidMin flinched at the thought of her dragging the Fleet First into a political *ui'DmukNa*-fest in the Chamber of Ancients, and he didn't need to be a telepath to see she'd do it. "There may be a backup position, if you want." He showed her the thick bundle of documents he carried. "We've been handed a new top priority assignment. There's a report of a possible new contact clear across our space near VebRin'deggg Great Nest colony. To hear it said, things haven't gone smoothly thus far. We're prepping our herd to head out on a patrol ship in a few days, as soon as the human herd arrives." He gave her an earnest look. "We could use your help."

His aura said his interest in her was more than simply official, which made her wary. "This is your backup plan? I go stampeding off across the Universe hoping to impress the Fleet First?"

"It would keep you from having to return groundside, and the more you accomplish, the better your chances for that Writ." He didn't add ("And it'll keep you from starting a stampede which could cost us all our ears"). Instead he offered an imploring ear twitch. "You have a unique talent which makes our Contact Herd work. You could do some real good out there, which can't help but be noticed in the World Nest."

He was right about that: the more she achieved, the better her odds. It would be a challenge...but it was important...and a life of useful purpose had a lot of appeal after her aimless existence on the street. She had to admit, reflecting on it, this was likely her one real hope. Even if she got her Writ, she was still a mentally altered misfit who would never blend in. For that matter...she was used to being a telepath by then...she knew she would miss having that edge. And even if she got her Writ of Forbearance, what would she do with herself groundside? She had no education, and the odds were she'd never fit in with the common herd. Maybe this —a life among the close-knit elite of the Contact Herd, along with Lieutenant Horton and the eccentric Sergeant MacIntosh—maybe this was her first, best destiny after all.

And K'nidMin took a *personal* interest in her. "Is it a long way from here? Will we be gone long?"

"It's clear across our stellar sphere, fifty days even on a fast ship. From there, we'll have to find these supposed aliens and make contact with them. I'd say this could take a year or more."

That would put her a long way from the Law on d'enchia, a long way even from the displeasure of the Fleet First. Based on her experience thus far, this new adventure would be difficult and dangerous...but no worse than a penal nest, surely.

Actually, on second thought, this life didn't sound so bad at all. Galloping around the Universe in good company, putting her abilities to good use, meeting more of those ten thousand alien races; that would beat d'enchia all hollow.

And there *were* aliens out there she was sure; enough alien races to keep her busy for a lifetime. What would their thoughts feel like, she wondered? She used to dream of travel and adventure in exotic, far-away places: one would have to go a long way to find more exotic adventures than what she'd already experienced. And K'nidMin's interest didn't displease her. Her Passage To Maturity was coming up soon...perhaps...

"So?" she said in feigned disinterest. *'Always keep him guessing,'* her mother said. "When do we leave?"

*****

"Postscript"
A Year Later...

"J J? J J Ballas? Can you hear me?"

'Ah'm right here, Lil-Missy.' The Dreamsinger's aura filled the small compartment with his warm unseen presence.

"Can you help me, please?   I need to contact my mother. Could you show me how?"

'Why, sho' nuff, Lil-Missy. Ah'm happy to oblige.'

The next few minutes went to tuning out the endless systems noises and the mental voices of the crew of ship 208.   Then J J showed her how to find another mind hundreds of light years away on a crowded planet.   It wasn't easy, but she finally grasped it. *'There you go, Lil-Missy.'*

She offered a quick thank you, then reached out to d'enchia, lost amid the distant stars. *'Mother? Can you hear me?'*

The compartment faded, and she felt an image of C'traBenla in her mind. She sensed surprise and confusion. *'R'nemReth?'*

'Yes mother, it's me.'

'It's good to hear from you! Are you in orbit yet?'

'No. Actually, I'm calling from clear across our stellar sphere; beyond it, in fact, out in unexplored space.'

She felt a sense of surprise and amazement. *'Your powers have grown, youngling. How are things aboard your new ship?'*

'They're great!   This ship is exactly what the Contact Herd needs.   But I didn't call to talk about the ship.   I have some important news for you.'

'What's that, dear?'

'K'nidMin and I...we're going to have an egg. You're going to be a...what do the humans call it?'

'A grandmother? This is wonderful, dear!'

'We're headed back to VebRin'deggg Great Nest colony for a refit. We'll give the egg to the crèche there.'

That produced a hint of regret. *'I don't suppose I'll be able to track the hatchling from this distance.'*

'I should hope not!   Our hatchling needs to grow up in a normal atmosphere without its Ancestors constantly interfering.'

173

Then she felt a sense of concern, even alarm.   *'But your egg...you were exposed to the Dreamsingers' powers while I carried you; what will your powers do to your hatchling?'*

'The feeling among our herd is this could be the start of our people becoming a true stellar species. If I can contact you from this distance, imagine what this egg means for the future!'

Uncertainty, and doubt.   *'That's a sobering thought, dear. I suspect your hatchling will not have a normal life.'*

'Probably not. But what is normal any more?'

'Sometimes I haven't the foggiest clue. Well...perhaps it's for the best. What about your search? Any luck yet?'

'We still haven't made contact, but we found more discarded trash orbiting another world. It's our third find; they seem to be surveying the region. We'll meet them eventually.'

'I'll pass that along to your father, with your personal news.'

'Has he forgiven me yet?'

'Yes. Your Writ of Forbearance finally came in.'

'Its about time!' she thought to herself.   *'That's great, mother. Please thank him for me.'*

'I guess I should go. Your father will be home soon.'

'Please give him my best. And I'm sure E'draMinr would want me to say hello, too.'

'How is your brother, dear?'

'Busy, with how the spaceport is growing. But he still has time to be a l'cc'vn knot in my tail.'

'You should learn more about human siblings, dear. Good bye for now.'

'Good bye, mother.'

The mental image faded, leaving the bare walls of their compartment, the endless hum of the ship's systems, and the muted presence of the crew. After a bit, she switched off the light over their bed and pulled the cover up over her head.

"Good night, J J," she mumbled. "Thank you."

'G'night, Lil-Missy. You take good care of the future, hear?'

*****

The End

Addenda:

Ic'nichi phrases:

A knot in one's tail
  A vulgar expression; slang for any annoying person or problem.

Ancestors
  The Ic'nichi do not raise their young as humans do; surrendering the newly laid eggs to the crèches shortly after delivery.   Since they do not have family ties, a common religious belief is that their unknown Ancestors watch over them.   Upon death, they are reunited with their Ancestors if they are judged worthy of joining their blood line.

Back of the Herd, the
  To have low seniority or rank; to be insignificant; to be looked down upon; slang term for a clueless newcomer.

Chamber of Ancients
  The Ic'nichi world government, a Parliamentary system with representatives of all the Great Nests. The seat of government is the World Nest, the capital circle.

Chasing Their Own Tails
  Slang term for desertion, incompetence, cowardice.

Circle
  Ic'nichi term for any organized social unit, both cities and towns, as well as offices or groups organized for a task.

Crèche (lower- middle- upper-)
  The Ic'nichi raise their young in crèches from when they hatch to maturity. These serve as residential schools providing the equivalent to a high school education. Most young Ic'nichi go on from there to advanced schools as independent adults.

Dark Grays, the
> The 'Dark Grays' are the Ic'nichi space fleet, answering directly to the Chamber of Ancients.

Defenders of the Nest
> Modest military forces raised by the various Great Nests, mostly involved in disaster relief and security duties. Defender services are named for the colors of their uniforms, for example, the 'Brown-And-Tans'.

Ear-fallen
> To be dismayed, depressed or heart-broken.

Ears-back
> To become confrontational or angry.

Echelon
> A military ground unit of roughly one hundred, equivalent to a human company.

Egg Testers
> Crèche workers who test newly laid eggs for genetic defects, and break the defective eggs with a small hammer, the symbol of their office; referenced as a symbol of fear, similar to the human BoogeyMan.

First Finger
> A common slang term among the Ic'nichi, which refers to their four mutually opposed fingers: the highest quality is 'first' (index) finger, followed by 'second', 'third', and finally 'fourth finger'; barely passing. The human equivalent are grades 'A', 'B', 'C', and 'D', respectively.

Forum
> A court of law, generally similar to human courts.

Great Nests (also Nests)
> Ic'nichi term for city-states composed usually of a major urban center (the Great Nest) and outlying towns (Nests).

Grunt

Authority; influence; political connections; the ability to persuade, especially with one's superiors.

Hand (hand's worth)

Four; the basic informal unit of measure based on the Ic'nichi's four-fingered hands.

Herd

The Ic'nichi evolved from herd beasts, and often use the term to refer to any group of people.

I'll have his ears

A euphemism for castration.

Lengths

Body length from snout to tail, about two meters, a common unit of informal measure.

Peace Wardens — Civilian Police.

Scale polishing —

Slang term for currying favor with one's superiors; generally thought of as disgraceful behavior; comparable to the human phrase 'sucking up'.

Service Wardens — Military police.

Tail knot

Slang term for anything annoying, perplexing or frustrating.

Tail-shaker

A prominent figure, someone of vast importance.

The set of his ears

Refers to the involuntary movements of Ic'nichi cat-like ears, indicating their emotions; euphemism for secret thoughts.

Tossed in tail-first

Slang term for doing a foolish thing; to find one's self in an impossible situation; to be abused and put-upon.

Uttermost Darkness

Ic'nichi belief that if their Ancestors judge them unworthy to join their bloodline after death, they will be cast out of the afterlife, dooming them to the formless void for eternity.

Worthy

A military rank comparable to a human sergeant.

*****

Ic'nichi words:

bv'nunma — A popular light meal similar to tuna salad.

cc'v'renk — Literally 'dishonored before ones' Ancestors'; acute embarrassment; disgraceful behavior; inability to make a decision; inability to see common sense; slang term for mental retardation.

d'enchia — The Ic'nichi home world.

er'trxxda — Literally 'haunted by the Ancestors' voices'; obsession; insanity; delusion; raging temper; vulgar habits.

hro'n'nad — Slang term meaning clueless or ignorant.

l'cc'vn — A vulgar adjective.

l'fru'ng — Brazen audacity; annoying habits; body odor.

l'ni'ddi — A popular fast food similar to stew.

M'mendoch — Literally 'someone who thinks fast'; slang term for a hustler; trying to get out of a hopeless situation; avoiding being cited by the peace wardens for a minor violation.

n'bna'nmn — Slang term for an idiot.

n'In'c — The most common Ic'nichi language, spoken by about 10% of their population.

n'vebRnng — Vulgar slang term for nothing, comparable to the human phrase 'we don't have squat'.

P'grrt'p — A small animal analogous to a field mouse known for its nervous nature.

p'quas'tka — A particularly vile obscenity.

r'fen'thi — An Ic'nichi ethnic group characterized by their physical size and a deep, coppery coloration.

riv'Agna — A mythical spirit, similar to an earthly 'demon'.

r'vebbe — Literally 'to feel one's Ancestors' disapproval'; slang term for being upset, shaken, or spooked by something strange.

'sti'eit — A popular brand of cheap liquor similar to ale, commonly served in service facilities.

t'pithm'ig — A showoff; an immature dandy; a vain person.

s'vem'grott — Vulgar slang term for being obstinate or stubborn; comparable to the human term 'pig-headed'.

uf'thoka — A popular vegetarian dish analogous to bean sprouts with a spicy garnish.

ui'DmukNa — Manure; slang term for anything stupidly offensive.

un'brapta — Cruel; heartless; self-centered; arrogant; the odor of unwashed linens.

un'tdar — A vulgar person; a pig-like animal; bad breath.

V'liz — A popular beverage containing a mild stimulant, which can be prepared either like coffee or soup.

'v'thorble — Slang term roughly comparable to 'hot rock'.

x'mnnb' — Literally 'dead fish'; slang for annoying, stupid behavior; comparable to the human term 'bullshit'.

*****

A Brief Note From The Author

Thank you for reading this novel, which is part of my favorite work of my writing. I hope it was a good read for you. I would love to hear from you, my readers, to let me know how I am doing as an author. Every bit of input helps me to make my next effort a better product for your enjoyment.

All my best,

Bob Boyd

You can learn more about me, and keep up to date on my efforts through our web site:

The Written Wyrd
http://www.the-written-wyrd.org/

*****

www.ingramcontent.com/pod-product-compliance
Lightning Source LLC
Chambersburg PA
CBHW072122170626
46813CB00004B/1659

* 9 780986 268083 *